NEW DIRECTIONS 48

In memoriam
ALFRED A. KNOPF
1892–1984

GEORGE OPPEN
1908–1984

Edited by J. Laughlin

with Peter Glassgold and Elizabeth Harper

Library of Congress Catalog Card Number: 37-1751

Unsolicited manuscripts must be accompanied by a self-addressed, stamped envelope and, in the case of translations, written permission from the foreign writer, publisher, or author's estate.

ACKNOWLEDGMENTS
Grateful acknowledgment is made to the editors and publishers of books and magazines in which some of the material in this volume first appeared: for Hume Croyn, *Ambit* (Great Britain); for Joan Retallack, *Interstate.*

Lars Gustafsson's "The Truly Great Strikes Wherever It Wants," a translation of "Det stora drabbar var det vill," was originally published in Swedish and included in the collection *Berättelser om lyckliga människor* ("*Stories of Happy People*"), P. A. Nordstedt & Söners Förlag, Stockholm, 1981.

"Ana and the Sea" ("Ana y el mar"), by David Huerta, is included in the poetry collection *Versión,* published by Fondo de Cultura Económica, Mexico City, 1978.

"The Amusement Park" ("Parque de diversiones"), by José Emilio Pacheco, is published by permission of Ediciones ERA, S. A., Mexico City.

Manufactured in the United States of America
First published clothbound (ISBN: 0-8112-0911-3) and as New Directions Paperbook 579 (ISBN: 0-8112-0912-1) in 1984
Published simultaneously in Canada by George J. McLeod, Ltd., Toronto

New Directions Books are published for James Laughlin
by New Directions Publishing Corporation,
80 Eighth Avenue, New York 10011

CONTENTS

CAN ZONE, OR THE GOOD FOOD GUIDE

RIKA LESSER

What do you mean, you "don't like poetry"?
Did someone force you, as a child, to taste
rancid stanzas, tainted, reeking lines, so poetry
made you sick (not at heart but) to your stomach? Poetry
laid on thick, like peanut butter, may take
its time dissolving on your palate. Poetry
thin as gruel's unpalatable. Still, poetry
made well, like a fine soufflé, will rise and stand.
How can I make a herbivore understand
that words are flesh *and* grass in poetry,
fish and fowl, birdflight, signs we read,
transforming themselves and us because we read?

Twelve years ago in the *Tribune* I happened to read
about GIANT BOLIVIAN FROGS. Of them I made poetry.
Frenchmen canned them, leaving enough to breed,
while chefs the world over steamed, roasted, grilled, and decreed:
No other known creature has such an unusual taste
or transmutable texture. And then the rumors spread:
*BIG FROGS RADIOACTIVE! THE DEVIL'S OWN EGGS! DRED-
GE LAKE TITICACA!* The strangest tales take
shape in poetry. Put down your *Times* and take
less heed of current events. In Ovid you'll read

how the will to change could help a girl withstand
indecent advances. See, by the pond, that stand

of laurels— "Croak!" blurts a frog. "Old myths don't stand
a chance in the—blouagh—modern world! Let's read
of true metamorphoses. Once we had to stand
in for a human prince; but our royal stand-
ard bore a crowned frog salient, King of Poetry!
Marianne Moore, who showed a firm understand-
ing of the natural order, took the witness stand
in behalf of our cousins (she had discerning taste):
In "imaginary gardens" (not really to our taste)
place "real toads"; they, warts and all, set stand-
ards for poetry. Subjects, be literal, take
us at our word. Nothing can be worth tak-

ing that serves but once. Amphibians always take
new leases on life; we are its double stand-
ard. Snakes shed their skins, but only we will take
ours off and eat them. Survive! Make no mistake,
on land, in water, you've got to learn to read
between the lines. Don't eat my words, take
them to heart: Leaps, turns, liberties, take
them all; change and be changed or poetry
will die!" Double-talk? Free speech? What else but poetry
encompasses so much? What else can take
bitter experience and camouflage its taste
so we may feed and live and breathe and taste

the next sunrise? What other art can make us taste
what we see: the golden egg whose rising we take
for granted, or set our sights on goose (tast-
ier still) all at once, prodding our taste
buds (smell those cracklings!), forcing our senses to stand
up and take notice? What else awakens taste
for the fruits of knowledge or plants an aftertaste
of first things in apples bitten and apples read?
What but this art can keep our daily bread
from going stale in our mouths?

"To each his taste,"
you say; "I'm hungry and all this talk of poetry
won't fill my gut!" —That only proves poetry

's power of suggestion. "But what if poetry
still gives me indigestion?" —A little taste
will surely settle the question. "What do you take
me for, a guinea pig?" —A hungry child who can't stand
being fed. The world's your oyster. Open wide, now. Read.

THE DECLINE OF SPENGLER

JOE FRANK

1

Hoffman died today—during surgery to remove fatty deposits from his thighs. Remember when we first met on the flight from Palestine. Gazing about us at smug, well-dressed tourists with expensive cameras, digital watches, calculators, and electronic beepers, we agreed that science had deprived most of the world of its gods, religions, its sense of meaning and permanence. Dostoevsky, Hoffman added, had seen the emptiness inherent in atheistic materialism and had opposed advances in technology that would lull the human soul into a sleep of material comfort, thus banishing from it a tragic sense of life.

I gazed out the porthole. Light and dark came out of the sky, I said. The sun, the moon, and the stars made their way across it. Nourishing rain fell from it. Rainbows glorified it. The awe with which ancient peoples had looked upon these phenomena was reflected in their religions. Rooted to the ground, they saw the sky as the home of angels and gods. I recalled Elijah ascending in his chariot of fire; Icarus, his wings beating, rising heavenward.

We looked back at the other passengers, who were reading catalogues, listening to cassette players, playing cards and talking . . . and we drank a toast to the past. Later, precooked chickens in

The Decline of Spengler was broadcast in dramatic form on National Public Radio's NPR Playhouse in April 1983.

wine sauce were handed out. We ate them, gazing at the stewardesses who were glamorous, courteous, friendly. They brought us desserts, mints, coffee, magazines, pillows, and blankets. They smiled, leaning over us, as if we were both their children whom they cared for with a steadfast, though indiscriminate, love. When one of them disappeared, momentarily, in a lavatory, Hoffman unfastened his seatbelt and followed her. When she unlocked the cubicle, he forced his way in, closing the door behind him. He was bored, he told her, and lonely too. In the brief struggle that followed—against a background of canned music—her arm dropped out of its socket, her head fell off, and he found himself holding a starched empty uniform, screws, nuts, bolts, coils of tubing, and electrical wiring scattered on the floor. He hurriedly cleaned up, stuffing everything into the towel dispenser . . . then returned to his seat, shaken. Later, we were told it was time for the evening movie: a popular children's adventure set in Berlin in 1936. The lights dimmed. People adjusted their headphones. I tilted my chair back, closed my eyes, and tried to sleep.

We were forty-thousand feet in the sky, traveling six hundred miles an hour, somewhere over the Atlantic.

A dream. I heard a fist beating sharply on the front door. I lifted myself wearily from the bed, put on my robe and slippers and, with the oil lamp in my hand, made my way into the foyer. I was exhausted. But I was the only doctor in the district and had no choice but to answer the door, hitch up my team of horses, climb into my wagon, and ride, sometimes for days, through a labyrinth of cobblestone roads until I finally reached my journey's end. And by that time, the patient had usually died anyway, having been buried so long ago that he was now only a dim memory.

I unbolted the door. Before me stood a man in livery. A few words were spoken, and I hurried back into the bedroom to change into my clothes. Soon I was racing along in a carriage. I could hear a whip cracking and the cries of the coachman urging the horses on. As we began the ascent into the hills, I gazed back at the sleeping village as if for the last time. An operation must be performed tonight. What had the coachman meant? I was bewildered yet felt, somehow, a sense of elation.

The carriage passed over a bridge and drew to a halt in front of a palace. I was led through the entrance, down a long corridor, and up a marble staircase. The coachman halted at an engraved, oak door. He knocked. A feeble voice called for us to enter. I walked into the room. The old man was lying in a huge, canopied bed. He was bald, toothless. His fingers trembled with palsy. He lifted a rag and retched into it. Then he looked up at me with a not unfriendly smile. I put my bag down beside the bed and called for a basin of warm water. The old man reached into my bag, drew out my surgical instruments one by one, and stared at them with fascination. Then the coachman told me to take off my clothes.

2

Hoffman's funeral was modest. A few people came to the chapel for a brief eulogy, then drove out to the cemetery. Earlier in the day, I'd visited Hoffman's apartment. In his journal, I'd found a map of Florida with x's marking spots where, according to different legends, the Fountain of Youth might be hidden. The Everglades, Fort Lauderdale, and Dreamland, the amusement park in Orlando, were cited. Also, I'd read Hoffman's notes on the latest advances in organ transplants, deep freezing, and high-speed space travel to prolong life. I was surprised. I'd had no idea of Hoffman's obsession. We gathered around the grave, by the ocean. I gazed out at the old people on the beach.

BORIS. Nice day, huh?

JACOB. Last week there was a wonderful day.

BORIS. What day was that?

ESTHER. Wednesday.

JACOB. Yes, Wednesday.

BORIS. There was no day last week that was nice.

JACOB. Not a cloud in the sky.

ESTHER. Did you sit outside?

BORIS. Too cold.

JACOB. It wasn't cold. What are you talking about?

ESTHER. It was not too cold on Wednesday. I know that.

BORIS. It was too cold last week. Now *this* week—today—this is a . . .

ESTHER. This is what you call a perfect day.

The day after Hoffman's funeral, I boarded a boat for a tour of the Everglades. We made our way slowly through a bubbling, frothing swamp choked with vegetation, great winged lizards hovering above us. We passed villages of semisubmerged dwellings where Indians sat up to their shoulders in water baking bread and assembling parts of tropical fish. Others kept herds of sheep and cows. But this was very difficult in the swamp, entire families employed in treading water and holding animals above their heads to prevent them from drowning.

A few days later, I took a bus to Fort Lauderdale, the second location marked on Hoffman's map. I arrived during the Aryan Convention. The hotels were filled with European and American delegates. The theme of the conference was the evolving history of Western civilization. There were lectures, exhibitions, and meetings. Each evening's entertainment was memorable: Monday night it was the New York Philharmonic; Tuesday evening, the Royal Shakespeare Company; Wednesday, the entire Ringling Brothers, Barnum & Bailey Circus performed; Thursday, the Ice Capades; and, on Friday, the highlight of the series—an epic film of Alpine country, with stretches of fragrant pine trees . . . picturesque farmhouses and chalets . . . cattle grazing in open meadows . . . fields of flaming Alpine flowers . . . and lakes whose unbroken perfect glasslike surfaces reflected towering mountain peaks. The film went on for hours. But no one was allowed to leave.

The following day was devoted to a demonstation of weapons. A bomb went off. And the next thing I knew it was dusk, I was lying on a mery-go-round in Miami Beach, my pockets had been turned inside out, and I was wearing a pair of fishnet stockings and pumps.

DR. ARNOLD. We have a human centrifuge we have built at considerable expense. The patients are placed inside it. The centrifuge is then activated, and the centrifugal force drives fluid to the outer walls of their arteries, thereby facilitating the flow of blood. Now when we prescribe a diet of foods that do not coagulate the blood . . . noncoagulating foods . . . clear soups . . . broths . . . fast moving foods, we call them, as opposed to fast foods, which we frown on . . . then if we put a male patient and a female patient in the human centrifuge, fill them chock full of fast moving foods, and ask them to seek fulfillment in each other—as the centrifuge is moving—we find that the combination of the fast moving foods and the centrifugal force clears not only their blood vessels and arteries, but also their nasal passages, the pupils of their eyes, their ears, and their hair seems to take on a remarkable lustrous quality. And, although this only lasts for as long as they're *in* the centrifuge, some people become mildly addicted to centrifugal activity. In fact, there are a few houses that have been built that are basically living modules that revolve so that one gets accustomed to living constantly with centrifugal force.

Another dream. A murder had been committed. The trial was in progress. I prosecuted the case myself. The evidence—a cup of vinegar, some thorns, fragments of wood, a few nails, and a pair of sandals—lay on a table in the courtroom. I cross-examined four witnesses. Each presented damaging testimony against the defendant who, wearing a black hat and a caftan, studied a legal tome. But it wasn't the defendant's scholarship that disturbed me. Rather, the jury—a motley group of shamans, sorcerers, prophets, and holy men—each one awaiting trial on charges of murder himself. Every morning they were led into the courtroom chained together. They sat in their chairs mumbling, deep in thought. They had the wasted, faraway look of fanatics. To make matters worse, the judge seemed to have withdrawn into his own world. Every few minutes he would look up, inquire as to the correct time, ask to be reminded of the general nature of the case before him, and call a recess to have the plastic bag, attached to his body, flushed out. The attending nurse rolled his wheelchair from the room.

That night, at the dinner table, I didn't know what to do. I was trapped in a nightmare. The case was hopeless. The months of interviews, of compiling evidence, of exhaustive research had been in vain. I sipped my soup and ate two spongy dumplings. After swallowing them with difficulty, I bent over to pick up the napkin that had fallen from my lap—and noticed my father sprawled in the hallway between the bedroom and the kitchen. His pajama pants had been drawn down to his ankles and, lying beside him, were a pair of pruning shears. I could barely stifle my laughter.

3

Received a call from a Mrs. Waterman. She said a mutual friend, who wished to remain anonymous, had suggested we meet. Then she recited a few facts about me to prove she hadn't picked my number from a phone book. I was suspicious. I knew someone might try to draw me into a compromising situation to discredit me. I'd heard, often enough, of how politicians were undermined or blackmailed . . . a pretty girl sent to them in the guise of a stranger on the street or an office worker who presumably fell in love with them and seduced them . . . at which point photographs of the event would be produced in lurid detail. She described herself as vivacious, beautiful, and sensitive. She said she was a gestalt therapist, a potter, and composed poetry. She was sure we'd enjoy each other. I wondered, then decided to take a chance. So we made a date.

The next evening I took a train to Rio David, where she lived. Two minutes after I arrived at the station, she drove up in a Mercedes sedan. I gazed through the windshield at a very attractive middle-aged woman with gray-blonde hair and a little Cupid's bow mouth. I got in and sat down beside her. She asked about the trip, remarked on the humidity, and we talked with ease. But I couldn't help noticing, as we drove along, the great black shroud of velvet that covered her almost entirely, the fabric extending robelike over her feet. I could see her face and the backs of her hands, but I couldn't make any sense of her body because the material was shapeless, jellylike. It would pucker at one point, then sag, then protrude at another. Her hair, which had looked natural and free through the windshield, seemed almost metallic, and her face was so rouged and painted that I began to wonder if the perfection of her nose and the height of her cheekbones were not merely artfully applied stage makeup. She asked me to look in her bag for her cigarettes. I opened the clasp and dozens of old, faded photos of her as a cheerleader, a beauty queen, a dancer, and a fashion model spilled out onto the seat. I rummaged through more old photos until I finally found a pack of Kents. I lit one and put it in her mouth. She sucked on it, her cheeks hollowing, and stared ahead.

Then she suggested we go to a motel nearby. We could talk more comfortably there. She said she'd get the room and prepare herself while I waited in a restaurant across the street. Then, after twenty minutes, I could join her. Her plan sounded odd, but I'd come too far to turn back. So she dropped me off at a kosher deli and made a U-turn to the motel. I went in, ordered a cup of tea, and took a table by the window.

When the twenty minutes were up I walked across the street. The man at the desk gave me the number of her room. I walked up a flight of stairs and down a corridor until I came to her door. I knocked. She called for me to enter. I turned the knob and went in. She was lying down, the covers drawn up to her neck. I walked by her to the window, parted the drapes, and looked out at a grassy field with a few dying trees. I could hear traffic in the distance. A toilet flushed in the next room. I turned to her and noticed a pair of metal canes under the bed. I averted my eyes, looking around the room at lamps, cabinets, chairs, tables, the TV set. The surfaces were painted to look separate, like individual objects, but it was really one prefabricated continuous entity entirely made of transluscent plastic, the kind of plastic that's used for bus seats. It was clear the room had been poured, had set, and been dropped here. She asked me to come over to her. But I said, "Wait," and went into the bathroom. I drew back the shower curtain revealing a wheelchair in the tub. She called out to me again, urgently. I tried to gather my wits. Then I said, "I can't do this. I'm sorry. It was a mistake. I have to go." But when I opened the front door, a gust of wind blew my toupee back into the bedroom. It landed at the foot of the TV. I stood there, immobilized.

MRS. WATERMAN. Come on, pick it up. Pick up your rug. You think you're too good to make love with me, huh? You think because you can stand on two feet and you don't need crutches or anything, you're a great big man, you're wonderful, huh? You're too good to get into bed with me. Well let me tell you something: a few years ago—before this happened to me—I wouldn't have spat on you! Well, go ahead. Pick it up and get out of here! I'm sick of looking at your stupid bald face! I can't move. I'm not going to jump on you and rape you. Don't worry. Just walk over there and pick up your hair. And put it on your head. And just get out!

There's a beach on the Gulf Coast scattered with fossils, where you can find saber-tooth tiger remains, parts of mastodon skulls, ancient shark teeth. The retired people go out on the sand at dawn to collect them. It's their consuming passion to find old bones. They save them, they catalogue them, they look them up in books to figure out what they are, they photograph them, they mail the photographs back and forth, they write learned notes, they form societies.

BORIS. I think it's very high. I think it must be at least ninety today.

JACOB. Yeah, the humidity is high.

BORIS. See the sweat on the plants? That's how you can tell. When the plants start to sweat.

JACOB. Also, the clouds. You can tell how humid it is . . .

BORIS. Those are not rain clouds. Those are not humidity clouds.

JACOB. I didn't say they were rain clouds, Boris. I said the humidity . . .

BORIS. . . . That's not true. Sometimes it can be a perfectly clear day and there will be high humidity . . . I'm telling you . . . the humidity is very high. That's all I can tell you.

4

Again, a dream. I woke up in a study. The walls were lined with rows of old manuscripts and ancient scrolls. A lamp on the night table glowed dimly. I lifted myself from the bed and walked to the bureau mirror. Staring back at me was a bearded middle-aged man with earlocks, wearing a black coat and hat. What's going on? I thought. What's happened to me? I threw the hat across the room and tugged violently at my beard—a shower of flaky crumbs falling at my feet. But it would not come loose. Then I began to run toward the bathroom, unbuttoning my coat, hoping to find a razor. But the voice of my housekeeper, Hilda, brought me back to my senses. "Just slide it under the door," I called. The letter was terse. The camps—steadily filling up—were at the bursting point. I'd been commissioned to design the new chambers and adjoining furnaces. The blueprints were long overdue. There was no more time to be wasted. I must, therefore, catch the next train for headquarters with whatever designs I'd completed, or face dismissal and a departmental trial. The letter was signed by Kummel himself. I read it over again and dropped it in the wastebasket. Then I changed into my uniform and had Hilda call me a cab.

The train was thirty minutes early—an example, I thought, of efficiency raised to the level of a paradox. The men of the railroad should be congratulated for their devotion to the future. I climbed aboard.

The car was crowded with men, women, and children who were wedged in so tightly that no one could move. I listened to the hum of their conversation, which seemed in an ancient, guttural tongue, and stared uneasily through the mist of cigarette smoke.

The rhythmic clicking of the rails made me drowsy. I congratulated myself on having found a safe niche in the corner, on the floor, which was covered with straw and random mounds of manure. It was an outrage, of course. That commuter service should deteriorate to this level. Then it occurred to me that I didn't know where I was going. I couldn't remember, either, when I'd boarded the train. I'm losing my mind, I thought. I'm so far gone that I've taken to boarding trains bound for districts in which I don't live. And if that weren't bad enough, I've selected an overcrowded car with no windows, with straw for seats, and piles of dung that are attracting horseflies by the dozens. And, as I said this, I swiped at one of them.

I woke up in a shower room. I was sprawled in an entangled pile of bodies. I peered out and saw a young man loading a wheelbarrow with the dead. I allowed myself to be tossed, like a doll, into the barrow. With my arm trailing in the dirt, I enjoyed the bumpy ride to the trench. It reminded me dimly of wagon rides in childhood. I was dumped on a heap of corpses and waited for the worker to go back to the chamber. Then I searched for a familiar face, a friend or an acquaintance. I saw the violinist, Jakov, lying nearby, his arms and legs twisted grotesquely. Next to him I recognized a streetcar conductor with whom I'd sometimes talked on my way to work. The man, after pleading with the guards, had been allowed to keep his cap, which was still set at a rakish angle on his head. There didn't seem to be anyone else I knew, except for the fat man who resembled Rothstein, the financier, rumored to have had affairs with famous actresses and opera singers. He looked flushed and bloated, as if he might burst. I began to search for Rachel, my former neighbor Holstein's wife. Sometimes in the drawing room of her husband's apartment we'd flirted together. It had come to nothing. But I'd always wanted to see her naked. I scanned the bodies but could not find her.

That night I climbed over the side of the trench and escaped. I traveled north, toward the Bavarian Alps. Weeks later, I arrived at the retreat of the Redeemer, the Chosen One. When night fell I climbed over the wall, cut through barbed wire, crawled past machine-gun nests, artillery and antiaircraft installations. In the backyard I found the Messiah planting trees in the moonlight.

MESSIAH: *Here, give me a hand. Pick up that shovel. Don't stand over there! You're standing on one of my seeds! Watch where you stand, you fool!*
awful. What's happened to you? Your clothes are torn. You look as if you haven't slept for days. How dare you appear before me in
I'm awfully sorry. I'm such an emotional little thing. You look these rags! Look at yourself! It's a disgrace! It's outrageous! I am sorry. I forgot you came here on your own, through all these endless obstacles. I'm sorry, my son. I apologize. Even I, at times, am only human. Bless you, my son.

DR. ARNOLD. We have found that the soil here in Palm Beach is remarkably conducive to growth of all kinds. A patient buried up to his neck in a small garden, for example, his scalp watered carefully and tended carefully, then Mozart being played for him . . .

DR. AINSLEY. Can I mention one thing? We have buried people—although we have not done it that way. We have buried them head first in the soil and found that people will relax that way, in garden soil, using hypnotherapy techniques with a speaker apparatus in the ground. I think you've stumbled upon something you didn't realize: that people will relax in soil.

DR. ARNOLD. Yes. This is true. This is very true. They will become particularly relaxed, particularly peaceful. Their anxiety seems to be alleviated and hair growth does seem to occur. One of the problems that we do have, however, is that the growth is not just limited to the scalp.

MODERATOR. What about the problem of loss of hearing? How does it happen?

DR. ARNOLD. Basically, it's because people have heard too much by the time they reach the age of fifty. By the time they reach a certain age, they've heard enough. And rather than, as with some of these other problems, it's one of physical deterioration, here it's much more emotional. It's a problem of people saying, "I'm not going to listen anymore because everything I'm hearing is making me upset."

5

I read Hoffman's journal every night. The first entry of Book III began with the question: "I wonder what Oswald would think of this?" And what *did* I think of it? I didn't know. It was the outline for a play. Hoffman wrote:

"The production takes place in a church. As the audience filters into the pews, the atmosphere is heavily religious—resounding organ music, heavy odor of incense, a collection box passed from bench to bench. At 8 P.M. the lights dim, the curtains part, and we find Poole, the film critic, tossing fitfully in his bed. Unable to sleep, he lifts himself wearily and walks to his desk. He sits down and thumbs through an old review. Gazing dully at it, he's startled by the whistle of a passing train.

"The curtains close. Act 1 has been completed in just forty seconds. During the intermission, the audience is served bitter herbs, unleavened bread, and sacramental wine. While the food is handed out and eaten, the actor who plays the part of Poole furtively enters the orchestra from the rear. He finds an unoccupied seat and falls asleep.

"Act 2 begins as Poole awakens, now a member of the audience that just observed him on stage. He yawns, stretches his arms, and sighs. *It was only a dream.* The house lights dim, the curtains part, and a movie is projected on a screen.

"The film is about a man who has lost his memory. Waking up in a field one summer afternoon, wearing only a gown and a pair of sandals, he can not recall anything about his past."

MAN. Who am I? What is this place? Peasant woman . . . Have you ever seen me before?

PEASANT WOMAN. What? You? No.

MAN. Are you sure I don't look familiar to you?

PEASANT WOMAN. No, I don't think you ever came through these parts before.

MAN. Thank you very much. Maybe I'll try down in the valley . . .

"He makes the rounds of the local police stations and missing persons bureaus, vainly looking through files of photographs to identify himself. Then he wanders across the countyside, moving from village to village, stopping people who look vaguely familiar to ask them if they know who he is."

MAN. I was wondering. Do I look familiar to either of you?

SHOPKEEPER. No, I don't think I've ever seen you . . .

SHOPKEEPER'S WIFE. Who are you, anyway?

MAN. Well, that's exactly the problem.

SHOPKEEPER'S WIFE. Well, maybe you've seen us. But I don't know if we've ever seen you or not.

SHOPKEEPER. I don't think we ever saw you—ever.

"In the course of his travels, he has a series of adventures with lepers and cripples, all of whom he manages to cure with the hem of his skirt."

HANS (ringing bell). Make way. Lepers. Beware.

MAN. Excuse me. Do you know who I am?

HANS. No, I don't think so.

MAN. Well, bless you both.

MARIE. I'm cured!

HANS. What's happened?

MARIE. Look, Hans! Your nose, it's coming back!

HANS. And you look beautiful! Oh, thank you.

MARIE. Thank you, kindly.

HANS. It's a miracle!

"Finally, sitting on a fence at the edge of a dirt road, he reviews his situation. He does not know his own name. He does not know where he came from. He does not know where he is going. And he does not know, moreover, what he is doing in this dismal film, so heavily symbolic, its themes of alienation and estrangement, with religious overtones, so painfully obvious."

MAN. There really must be some other way for me to solve my problems. There has got to be a way out. All right. I know what to do.

"He shakes his head, disgusted, steps out of the screen, and walks up the aisle toward Poole."

MAN. Ladies and gentlemen. I can't explain now. I'm sorry to disturb you. But I'm sure everything will be fine. I had to leave that film . . .

"Poole is suddenly terrified. He's just seen art impinge itself on reality. How can someone step out of a movie screen and into real life? Sensing a plot, Poole draws out his Luger and fires."

"The man crumples to the floor. He moans, shakes convulsively, and dies. Poole rushes up and looks at the body, which seems to be deflating, blood running from its mouth. *What have I done*? he cries. He races up the aisle and dashes up a marble staircase to the projection room. The projectionist, a little boy with pink cheeks and wings, looks up from his magazine."

POOLE. Excuse me. Little boy . . .

BOY. Oh, mister. You're not supposed to be in here.

POOLE. Little boy, can you please stop this film and run it backward?

"Poole asks him to reverse the film. In doing so, he hopes to suck his victim back into the screen, to restore his life."

BOY. Gee, mister, I don't know what to do.

POOLE. What do you mean, you "don't know what to do"? Aren't you the projectionist?

"The scene is televised and relayed to the audience through monitors at both sides of the stage.

POOLE. Do you have a supervisor or somebody?

BOY. Do you want to talk to the manager?

POOLE. Yes, the manager. Where is the manager?

BOY. Oh, he's in the manager's office.

POOLE. Well, where *is* the manager's office?

BOY. You step out in the hall. Make your first left. Go up the flight of stairs. And it's about your fourth door . . .

"Poole rushes out and begins running up the spiral staircase. Gasping, he finally reaches the door of the manager's office. He knocks. There's no answer. He tries the knob and the door swings open. The room smells of decay. Poole, his hand clasped over his mouth and nose, plunges forward until he comes upon the carcass of an old man, sprawled on the floor, his eyes and mouth open.

"Downstairs, in the theater, the curtains close. A small crowd forms around the body, which still lies in the aisle. Someone breaks down sobbing, another cries shrilly for an ambulance, a third runs out to the lobby to find a phone and call the police. Each one, however, is an actor playing a role. The audience, now assured that positive action is being taken, settles down to Act 3.

"In Act 3 we find Poole hermetically sealed in a phone booth. He dials numbers and speaks to people, but we can't hear anything he says. Perhaps he's consulting his lawyers. Perhaps he's speaking with members of his family. Perhaps he's dialing at random and conversing with anyone who will talk to him. The audience is left in doubt. We can only watch his facial expressions and gestures, his mouth shaping the contours of words we can't quite make out. During Poole's dumb show a heated discussion progresses on center stage. The panel is composed of robed clergymen who debate the responsibility for Christ's martyrdom."

FATHER BLUNT. Was Christ's martyrdom in fact a real martyrdom, since he rose again? It is a difficult question in law.

BROTHER THEOBALD. Well, truly, in lines 31–57 it says "Though he rise again, be he still dead, among us he shall walk." Christ did not plan to become a martyr. He did not say, "I shall become a martyr." So you see it's not born into the man as he will be risen later, but actually as he rises himself, he proves himself.

BISHOP BOYLAN. I think this is all true. Father Bartholemew raises another point.

FATHER BLUNT. On the other hand, we must consider that celibacy has always existed as an idea in the church . . .

"The argument soon gets derailed, sliding into tangential questions concerning celibacy, priestly habit, the superiority of certain wines."

FATHER BLUNT. The ideal has always existed.

BISHOP BOYLAN. Ah, yes. But the ideal has no meaning anymore. Practice is all. What are we here for but not to practice?

BROTHER THEOBALD. Brothers, this is not a discussion of Platonic concepts of ideals . . .

BISHOP BOYLAN. Precisely.

BROTHER THEOBALD. It's not a question of the caves. This is a question, though a man be risen, can he be said to be a martyr.

BISHOP BOYLAN. Yes, Doctor O'Malley was right when he said that martyrs cannot exist if they do not enter into the mainstream of contemporary civilization. When we are spoken of as men of the cloth, I think the tailoring of our habits should be considered as important as the tailoring of our ideals.

BROTHER THEOBALD. Man is known by the raiment he doth put on.

FATHER BLUNT. Indeed. It is what they called *illustratio ad ves-*

titudine. Or, if you will, *vestitudine sine vestitu* in the case of one who goes without cloth. So we must be with the cloth and of the cloth . . .

BISHOP BOYLAN. Yes, by the cloth, of the cloth . . .

BROTHER THEOBALD. And through the cloth I think we shall succeed.

BISHOP BOYLAN. Look! There are wine stains all over your gown! It's an abomination! Why in the world don't you wear those wash-and-wear gowns we've been speaking of all these times?

BROTHER THEOBALD. Father, I'm not so vain as to . . .

BISHOP BOYLAN. You are a slob.

BROTHER THEOBALD. You are an idolator!

FATHER BLUNT. You can't tell a Chateauneuf-du-Pape from sherry.

BISHOP BOYLAN. A Châteauneuf-du-Pape is a very sarcastic wine with a terribly bitter aftertaste and a not very confident bouquet.

BROTHER THEOBALD. A small nose. A wine of very small nose and of a presumption.

FATHER BLUNT. I take great offense . . .

BROTHER THEOBALD. It has no finesse!

"The audience, at first intrigued, but now bored, begins to file out of the theater. The remaining few are rewarded for their patience, however, with an organ recital. The music drowns out the clerics who, unable to reason any longer, engage in a violent struggle for dominance. Poole laughs uproariously. Perhaps he has just heard something witty over the phone. Perhaps he is amused by the priests' slaughter. Perhaps he is laughing at the awful silence of the universe. We watch him grip his belly, his body bent forward, shoulders jerking convulsively, tears streaming down his face—which is buried now in his cupped hands—as the curtain closes for the third and final time."

SICK WOMAN (*through telephone*). Hello.

DOCTOR AINSLEY. Hello.

SICK WOMAN. Doctor, listen.

DOCTOR AINSLEY. Yes.

SICK WOMAN. I am wearing a neck brace.

DOCTOR AINSLEY. Yes.

SICK WOMAN. I had a freak accident.

DOCTOR AINSLEY. Uhuh.

SICK WOMAN. When I bent down. And my bones are twisted on the left side.

DOCTOR AINSLEY. Uhuh.

SICK WOMAN. I have to be on Valium all the time.

DOCTOR AINSLEY. Yes.

SICK WOMAN. Because I have fast heartbeats of a hundred and thirty-five beats a minute.

DOCTOR AINSLEY. Yes.

SICK WOMAN. Which my heart could bust and I could drop dead of a heart attack.

DOCTOR AINSLEY. Well, what exactly is the problem?

SICK WOMAN. It's . . . ahh . . . breathing . . . heavy on the chest.

DOCTOR AINSLEY. Uhuh.

SICK WOMAN. Fast heartbeats. And a very nervous stomach.

DOCTOR AINSLEY. Yes. Go on.

SICK WOMAN. And I start to sweat and feel hot when it's not.

DOCTOR AINSLEY. Uhuh.

SICK WOMAN. And I feel cold when it's not.

DOCTOR AINSLEY. Uhuh. Yes. Go on.

SICK WOMAN. And I think like I'm dying and I wish I would die to end it all.

DOCTOR AINSLEY. Well, we're going to have to move along here. I appreciate your talking to me, but if we can't narrow in on the problem, we can hardly give you an answer.

BORIS. Ahh. Beautiful day!

ESTHER. I've got a headache.

JACOB. If only the humidity would let up.

BORIS. What do you mean? There's no humidity. Hey, it's so beautiful. It's a perfectly clear day.

ESTHER. You don't have any trouble with your sinuses?

BORIS. No. My sinuses are perfect. I'm in perfect shape. I just went to the doctor. The doctor said I have the heart and lungs of a twenty-five-year-old man.

ESTHER. So how long do you think you're going to live?

JACOB. Everything else is falling apart.

BORIS. If I die tomorrow, I'll still have better lungs than you do.

JACOB. While your lungs are okay, you want to play a little canasta?

BORIS. No, I don't like canasta. How about bridge? Anyone want to play bridge?

JACOB. It's a boring game.

BORIS. And canasta isn't?

JACOB. Canasta's got a little life . . . a little spunk.

ESTHER. What's wrong with bridge?

JACOB. It's a boring game.

6

Another dream.

I was a brilliant scholar, well versed in the subtleties of the Gemara and the complexities of the Kabbalah. Yet I remained a troubled man, bewildered about the course and purpose of my life. One evening, while contemplating suicide, I overheard two students speak fervently of the Zaddik of Rome. Perhaps this famous wise man possessed the answers I needed. In any event, I decided to go and see for myself if the master's teachings justified his reputation. I put on my hat, my coat, packed an overnight bag, and traveled on foot to Rome. When I reached the Zaddik's house and finally stood before him, I waited for the Zaddik to speak profoundly. But the Zaddik only told me that once a surgeon was called to a great house where an operation was performed on him. After this, he dismissed me.

I took a room for the night at a local inn.

The following evening I again went to the Zaddik's house. Surely tonight I would hear something of the master's wisdom. But all the Zaddik told me was that once a famous prosecutor found himself guilty as charged.

I did not know what to make of these parables.

When I returned to the inn, I collected my belongings, paid the bill, and hired a driver for the journey home. We would start as soon as the weather cleared. But around midnight, when the full moon came out, a man from the Zaddik burst in with a message for me. I was to visit the Zaddik immediately. I left at once. This time the Zaddik received me in his study. He told me that a great engineer awoke, one evening, in just such a room, and that upon ris-

ing and gazing into a mirror, he found himself transformed into a holy man. An official dispatch slipped under his door brought him back to his senses. The letter requested his immediate departure for headquarters. He caught the next train that passed through his provincial town only to find himself trapped in a car crowded with refugees bound for prison. He miraculously eluded death and escaped by cutting his way through barbed wire. Then he traveled north until he finally reached the retreat of the Messiah. The Messiah was planting trees in the moonlight.

Bewildered by this absurd and extraordinary story, I interrupted the Zaddik. "Why are you telling me this?" I asked. Staring fiercely at me, the Zaddik removed his outer garment revealing an S.S. uniform beneath and announced himself to be Captain Kreitz of the Secret Police. He scornfully placed me under arrest. Two soldiers entered and took me to a van parked at the curb. But on the way to the prison, the van was forced off the road, I was rescued by the Jewish Underground, and I was taken to the real Zaddik of Rome who, disguised as a Nazi officer, was vacationing in Palermo.

When we reached the Zaddik's house and I finally stood before the master—resplendent in a black uniform with a death's head, crossbones, and an Iron Cross—I waited for the Zaddik to utter the words of his teachings so that I might weigh them. But the Zaddik only told me that once a surgeon was called to a great house where an operation was performed on him. After this, he dismissed me.

I took a room at a local inn. All night long I labored at the blueprints for the chambers on my drawing board.

The next evening I again went to the Zaddik's house. But all the Zaddik told me was that once a famous prosecutor found himself guilty as charged.

I did not know what to make of these parables.

When I returned to the inn, I collected my belongings, paid the bill, and caught the next train for Berlin.

MESSIAH. *Little by little, time kills all our illusions. Pipes rust . . . paints peel off . . . arteries harden . . . brains soften . . . gums bleed . . . teeth rot . . . lovers leave . . . friends flee . . .*

What has become of us? We are no longer firm bright apples on the firm bright tree of life. We are a mess of rotting apple sauce.

A change has come over the world like a cloud.

Dark thoughts are born. Dark deeds ripen in the midst of their vapors. The eye of God no longer shines on us. Where once it shone there is nothing now but an empty, burned-out socket.

We are lost.

I'll buy a gas station or open a small TV repair shop in Tampa. I'll marry an attractive divorcee—a clerk in a department store selling beauty products. She'll be tired of sleeping with people in motels that are so well lit outside you can never get the room dark enough. She'll marry me because she'll want a stable home life. We'll sit in the backyard of our trailer on those chairs with straps on them, next to a chipped birdbath. We'll grow old together. Then, one day, I'll get a hernia when I'm fishing in my small boat and hook a cinder-block. I'll develop prostate trouble and get cancer of the nose. She'll become religious. She'll turn to Jesus—who has snake hips, is quite lean, blond, a pretty fair surfer, has a beautiful tenor voice, plays the pedal steel guitar, and would be a very fine dirt bike scrambler except for his robes.

She'll go to church in a slightly shiny blue suit with frills around the neck, a hat with a little bunch of cherries, a purse, gloves, and sensible high-heel shoes.

And there will be no mezuzah in our doorway . . . only the totemic pink flamingo, made of plaster of Paris, on our front lawn.

7

Cleaned out Hoffman's apartment yesterday. Gave most of his belongings to local charities. Kept a prayer shawl, some books of mysticism and poetry, a ram's horn, and a Hebrew Bible. Also uncovered, in the back of his closet, a neatly folded black uniform, a riding crop, boots, and a cap with the insignia of a lightning bolt. Hoffman's journal closed with a description of Dreamland, the amusement park in Orlando. The work going on at the space center there, he wrote, was extremely promising. In fact, he'd booked himself on the inaugural flight of its rocketship, rumored to be capable of unprecedented speed. I found the ticket in the back of the journal. I decided to drive up and see for myself.

In Dreamland. Strolling along the midway. I pass rides . . . exhibits . . . concessions. Then I see the spaceship poised on its platform. A crowd is gathered around it, listening to the speech of a tour guide.

TOUR GUIDE. The Floridian peninsula plays a large part in the history of world exploration and scientific discovery. What first attracted explorers to Florida was the legend of a Fountain of Youth. Soon, entrepreneurs and fortune hunters, as well as the old, sick, and dying, came here in search of the restorative spring. The Fountain was never discovered. But in its place this rocketship has been built that can transcend the speed of light and reverse the aging process. Tickets are available in both first class and coach . . .

I give Hoffman's ticket to the guard at the gate, walk up the ramp, and enter.

STEWARDESS. Flight 66 is now ready for departure. Please check that your seatbelt is securely fastened and your seat upright for lift-off.

MISSION CONTROL. Launch sequence. Five . . . four . . . three . . . two . . . one . . . ignition.

BLAST OFF

When I wake up, we've crash-landed in a swamp. The ship is a smoking ruin. We spend most of our time running, hiding, jumping from behind rocks, springing out of trees, emerging from holes in the ground, and dragging ancient and useless electrical household appliances behind us.

Yes, hundreds of years have passed into the future. We've learned there was a war, the concussions from nuclear explosions altering the earth's axis causing the polar icecaps to melt, flooding coastal areas so that New York, from which so many members of our group originally migrated to Florida, was buried three hundred feet under the ocean, fishes swimming in and out of the windows of the city.

And now the members of our expedition serve as the wise men and women of tribes and kingdoms. We write histories, books on ancient technology, and go on long hikes in the mountains, through fields of flaming Alpine flour, a cup of vinegar, some thorns, and a pair of sandals, and I dreamt I woke up dreaming again, or was I still awake dreaming I was asleep under a fountain with a tank of ice water, a spout, and a dispenser with paper cups, thinking: Listen, just bring me a mint, coffee, and a pillow, and I'll try to relax. Do you have any Dramamine? I think I'm out of my depths. You see, my problem is whenever I go to a funeral I don't know whether to laugh, cry, or demonstrate floral arrangements. I've failed to adopt a point of view over Palestine—or Miami, for that matter—is glorious. The shrines, the fossils, the history, the sheer incoherence of it all is a form of amnesia, like being trapped in a burning temple wearing a pair of shorts and suspenders and performing in a traditional folk dance, thinking: help *me* . . . save *me* . . . catalogue *me* . . . look *me* up in books to find out who *I* am . . . what *I've* done . . . and I'll say, "Thank you. Thank you very much. Very nice of you. I appreciate it. I really do. You have a kind heart. A good soul. I won't forget this. Ever again.

MESSIAH. *All this is not my fault. Nothing of it is my fault. I had nothing to do with it. I am in no way responsible. I'm not responsible! I said I wasn't there! None of this is my fault! I had nothing to do with all this! I AM INNOCENT! I AM TELLING YOU, I HAVE NOTHING TO DO WITH ALL THIS! I WASH MY HANDS! I WAS TOTALLY UNAWARE OF IT. I WAS TOLD ABOUT IT LATER! MUCH LATER!*

FIVE POEMS

JULIA THACKER

TAHITI 1897

After the painting *D'ou Venons Nous, Que Sommes Nous, Ou Allon Nous* by Paul Gauguin

Posed since the first good light
my left side sleeps.
Tahishna fans the madonna

with a cluster of feathers
and you say nothing
on her first well day.

Ill so long with measles
the holes in her ears bled
when we put the earrings in

this morning. During your last trip
she called for you at the shore
through a hollow coconut shell.

Felice, she mocks you, the name
you say in your sleep.
She has no French,

knowing all she can know
with the body.
Painter, you choose rose-madder

for thighs. On our faces, shadow.
On our tongues
the questions of the holy.

What are we?
The French missionaries
sprinkled the babies' heads,

remember?
The palm frond drifts far out to sea
and in this water, no forgiveness.

CITY NIGHTS

Diamonds spit and hiss.
They don't moan.
They don't remember bare hands
mining them from the mountain.
Freed diamonds!
Out of the mountain!
Strange, these evenings, ladies
in leopard prints, their ears
pierced with the earth's miseries.

PAY PHONE

for Vickie McElwee

In those days we had the leisure
of conversation over coffee.

Now I'm calling to say I'm lost
Have I done the right thing?
and we try to pour weeks
into three minutes.

We talk about the breakers
on this coast, how they begin
at the edge of Portugal
and wash up here, the same energy
and nothing can hold them.

Shouldn't this be a metaphor, you ask.

What do I know?
Not the velocity of waves
or if there is value
in the constant moving away,
whether worn coves of new lands
make us less than we are
or more.

Today I am only sure of the sand in my hair
and water
and water's desire for shore.

MAN CARRYING NO MONEY SLAIN IN HOLD UP

—headline, *The New York Times*

Take the black cloth from
the mirrors,
from the parakeet's cage,
I need a melody to whistle.
This mouth framed
too many goodbyes,
is full of pins as I hem
my Yocheved's black dress.

Two breasts, two blackberries
to stain her man with sadness.
I tell her,
Yocheved, go next door
and borrow the pearl necklace.
Also that nice swan ash tray
for the butcher
flaking ashes on my rug.
In the parlor they laugh
because the rabbi has bitten
a gold thimble in the cake.
And I cut fresh amaranth
to put in the guest room
for sorrow, our quiet boarder.

THE CARPENTER

On Sunday mornings (because everyone
at church was plotting against him)
he shadowboxed in the back yard,
jabbing dangerously
close to the brick wall.

I found the shirt with the orange palm trees
in the garage, after he left,
and wrapped the sleeves around me,
until Mother gave it for
the Goodwill; with a bobby pin
scratched his face off a photograph.

For the sake of white
we left cellophane on the lampshades,
I swear by the pit of the olive
we shaved our arm pits clean and
giggled in the bathroom,
dabbing Lily of the Valley Cologne

behind our knees
for Prayer Meeting, where
we knelt gently, having forgotten
a man's hard embrace.

Like Jesus,
I belong wholly to my mother.
Once a man scarred his knuckles,
from reticence, built us a house.

EIGHT POEMS

JAMES LAUGHLIN

ARE OUR NEUROSES

compatible my shrink says
that is necessary for a

happy relationship I am
afraid of all machines

especially the telephone
which is the lute of Lu-

cifer most girls are a-
fraid of mice snakes &

spiders please inform me
regarding any particular

anomalies and I'll do my
best to compensate I want

us to get on really well.

CAN I BATTER MY WAY

into your heart with words
being a classicist I use

only Greek typewriters my
old one was named Olymp-

ia and my new one is Her-
mes he is the messenger

of the gods he gets a-
round and hears things

he'll bring me a lot of sto-
ries that should amuse you.

CORDELIA

why couldn't you have
thought up just a few

kind words to say to
your dear old dad and

then we wouldn't have
to take all that crap

from Goneril & Regan
but if you had I sup-

pose then we'd never
have heard things like

the serpent's tooth &
the wanton boys killing

flies & the wrens going
to it (let copulation

thrive) & the ounce of
civet for my imaginings.

HOW SHALL I FIND MY WAY

to your forfended place what stra-
tagem of love will compass me that

joy it seems the artifice of words
has failed what must I now employ?

IS IT WRITTEN

in heaven that our planets
should conjoin the old as-

trologer in Madras who did
my horoscope said that in

1984 something sensational
would happen did he mean

you delicious creature I
hope I pray I do beseech

you that's what he meant.

THE NEEDLE IS STUCK

in the groove of the old record
and it just goes round and round playing the same bar
they are all writing the same way, the same old stuff
what they learned from those poets in residence
in the creative writing classes in college
or what they have painstakingly tried to copy from the pages
of the New Yorker
the same old stuff, only it isn't really music
it's just something a printer has set in type
and how would a printer know the difference
for that matter, does anybody know the difference

WHY WON'T YOU IGNITE

from the sparks of my lan-
guage delivered to your door

in a brazier by the boy Eros
whom I have engaged for the

purpose he is a costly mes-
senger (I have to fly him

down from Olympus) but for
you nothing can be too good.

YOU HAVE REPLACED

the Primavera in the gal-
lery in my head as well as

that lady whom nobody knows
what she is smiling about do

you Diana the huntress no
longer arouses my emotion

and Parvati stretching out
her hand to Lord Siva looks

like a buxom peasant girl
long is the list of those

whom you've displaced but
when will you move from my

head to some place warmer?

BLACKMAIL

JOYCE CAROL OATES

. . . my intense awareness of & deep rapport with Lew Chatwin was simultaneous with his interest in me though he was my elder (I should say *is*!—for of course C. lives still) by several years; & had already begun to acquire a reputation as an avant garde playwright (which he has subsequently betrayed by seeking to placate the Bitch Goddess Success). In one or another public place & later at the homes of mutual friends our glances began to meet, pleading & longing. . . . Our hands sought to clasp, our lips & thighs. . . . Velvet-soft was our yearning through months of restraint in a harsh winter of 20 years ago, though in the end Chatwin's desire swept all before it. & his steely hard & purposeful conquering *will*.

. . . after his 'violation' of me (for so despite my guilty complicity I came to think it: I was but 22 years old & laughably a virgin) I bled & bled & he grew alarmed & took pity (for it has always been C's way to feel *intense solicitude* where only minutes before he has been a ravening beast) & brought ice cubes wrapped in a towel to press against my poor torn bleeding flesh. . . .

. . . 'It isn't love,' C. declared,—flush-faced & angry & leonine in his swarthy splendor—'I forbid you to think so.'

—from "Fragments of a Life," by Oliver X.

Could you die of words, Chatwin wondered,—could words, lacking all substance, and in this particular case lacking even truth, *kill*? Sickened, trembling, he tried to console himself with the brave sing-song rejoinder of childhood, as old as the race, *Sticks and stones may break my bones but names will never*. . . .

Lewis Chatwin was forty-six years old and though he told no one otherwise, he really wasn't in the best of health. He had lived too intensely for too many years; he'd treated his body as impatiently and cruelly as his former wives might have charged him with treating theirs. Reading and rereading these fictitious memoirs by a former acquaintance, Chatwin felt rage suffuse him from within like steam. A terrible pressure in his chest, a pressure in his skull, veins and arteries swelling, the very envelope of his skin grown tight as if close to bursting. His distress was physical. It was immediately physical. The banal "poetic" language of his tormentor Oliver X. as lethal as a bayonet. . . . The man wants me to die, Chatwin thought, dazed and panicked; he wants me to read these loathsome things and *die*.

For days, for weeks, he thought about virtually nothing else: the pseudonymous Oliver X. (whom he'd known as Oliver Holland) who so hated him, so envied him, he wanted him dead. Did anyone else living take Lewis Chatwin so seriously?—would anyone else living have spent so much time concocting a fantasy in which "C." reigned as a monstrous hero? Then, one morning, too dispirited to work, he skimmed through Oliver X.'s poorly typed manuscript another time, and thought suddenly that the mystery behind it was really a very simple one: he was being blackmailed.

But how did a civilized person deal with a blackmailer. . . ?

Chatwin was a failed playwright whom careless people, even informed and intelligent people, mistook for a success. For a few years in his late twenties things had gone well for him, that was true: a number of gratifying awards, including a Drama Critics Circle award, one or two flattering profiles in national magazines. A long and very slow decline, however, began when he was in his mid-thirties, and had yet to bottom out. He worked desperately hard, he worked constantly, he took on every variety of short-term job offered him, with the consequence that the name Lewis Chatwin frequently surfaced in print, and perhaps explained some measure of the animosity felt for him in certain quarters. (He was now involved, for instance, in doing the script for Henry James's satirical fantasy, "The Private Life," which, if things went happily, would be produced by National Public Television.)

Through his career, of course, Chatwin had received highly disagreeable letters from time to time, letters from strangers that bristled with hatred and spite, and occasionally with a sort of radiant madness; he had drawn his share, perhaps a little more than his share, of professional venom, along with more reasoned (and more justified) criticism. But these utterly fictitious memoirs—these "Fragments of a Life" which Oliver Holland had dared to send around to New York magazines—were something entirely different. Reading them, rereading them, getting out of bed at four o'clock in the morning to skim them yet again—as, Chatwin thought, one might rise, and turn on the light, to examine with both fascination and dread a hideous growth that was gradually sapping his strength—Chatwin invariably experienced the same emotions: a sense of disbelief; a numbing sort of shock; commingled disgust, rage, shame. He was utterly ashamed, *ashamed.*

Copies of the malicious document were forwarded to Chatwin by several editors who were friends of his, or friends of friends; or who felt uneasy about the situation—after all, the writing was extremely frank, a sort of mad lush homosexual rhapsody; unpublishable in its present form; perhaps even unprintable. It was poorly typed with many erasures and emandations, and poorly photostated; accompanied by a very brief covering letter—"Herewith I submit for your consideration a manuscript I believe you will find highly interesting"—that had been photostated as well. The return address was Mt. Rose, New Jersey.

Fifty pages celebrating a love affair of two decades previous that had never happened—that had never, from Chatwin's side at least, even been imagined. He had no homosexual experience; he had no interest in it. He'd loved only women, to the extent to which (if he believed the accusations made against him) he had been capable of loving anyone at all. He was even the father of a fourteen-year-old boy who lived with his first wife in Minneapolis—not a very good father, he supposed, but a father nonetheless. Oliver X.'s fantasy figure "Chatwin" ("complex, manly, cruel & utterly rapacious") had simply never existed.

Though the narrative strategy of "Fragments of a Life" was lyric and episodic and not very coherent, a chronological pattern emerged: the virginal Oliver was seduced by Chatwin, subjected over a period of months to a variety of humiliations, surprises, and "ecstasies," and finally dismissed. He then suffered a nervous collapse, spent some time in what appeared to be a private hospital, made a precarious recovery ("which is precarious still, after 20 years"). The love affair took place presumably in Chicago, when Chatwin was teaching part-time, and working part-time for the *Tribune,* and trying to write the first of his ambitious plays—an extraordinarily intense and rather manic phase in Chatwin's life—but very little mention was made of that background; nor was there any mention of Chatwin's love affair with a young woman named Yvonne whom he eventually married. The male figures who drifted lyrically in and out of the narrative—"Todd," "Leslie," "Brock"—were wholly concocted.

One of the editors who had seen the material, and telephoned Chatwin about it, asked if "Oliver X." was anyone he had ever known. Chatwin said no. But it was clearly someone who seemed to know him, the editor said. And again Chatwin said *no.*

At about this time Chatwin was suffering from a mysterious rash on his forearm. In the beginning the skin raised itself into small worm-like welts; then it began to itch, at first mildly; then the welts became pimples, and pustules, and the itching was so terrible he dug at it with his fingernails and drew blood. Soon the rash had become a sort of lurid *bas-relief,* about four inches long and rhomboid-shaped, hot, yellow, throbbing as if with desire. . . . Chatwin spread some Noxema on it, bandaged it up, tried to forget it; tried not to scratch it. When he examined it a few days later he saw that it had turned a queer mottled rust color and had begun to form a scabby crust. Though it still itched violently he believed the scab must be a sign of healing.

He wondered if he had been blackmailed before in his lifetime and had forgotten about it. The sensation of commingled rage and helplessness was so familiar, after the initial shock. " 'It isn't love,' " he heard a voice declare, " 'I forbid you to think so.' " It was his voice but not Chatwin himself speaking.

Though Chatwin had the reputation for being short-tempered he was not in principle a violent man. He believed in a strong gun-control law; he wouldn't have a pistol in his apartment, though it had been broken into and burglarized several times during his six-year tenancy. (He lived on West Thirteenth Street on what he considered a quiet block.) But in preparing for his visit to Mt. Rose he thought he had better bring along a gun: not that he intended to threaten Oliver Holland, or even to show him the gun. The man might be dangerous and he didn't want to take any chances. So he borrowed a .32-caliber Colt revolver from a girl friend who said it probably wasn't in the very best condition because she had never used it and it had never been oiled. Chatwin told her that didn't matter—he didn't intend to use it either.

Chatwin rented a small white Ford and drove out to New Jersey one Sunday afternoon in early April. He didn't try to telephone "Oliver X." beforehand, though he had his number; he didn't want to alert him in any way. And if he got to the blackmailer's address and no one was there—Chatwin would have to accept that as a sign that nothing could be done. The very violence of his emotions had made him superstitious lately.

The revolver was in his valise with a bottle of Scotch and a copy of "Fragments of a Life." When Chatwin travelled he usually took a bottle of Scotch with him; it had become a comfortable, practical habit, it saved trouble. Though Mt. Rose wasn't far from Manhattan Chatwin didn't know exactly how long he would be away. He might check into a motel and stay overnight. . . . His plans were hazy, open-ended.

By this time the flurry of excitement over the magazine submissions had subsided; Chatwin hadn't received one of those embarrassed telephone calls, or another copy of the wretched memoir, in several weeks. But he knew enough not to be comforted—the blackmailer was probably sending his work to less scrupulous magazines by now; to gay publications of the kind Chatwin noticed sometimes on newsstands and displayed in the windows of marginal bookstores. He wondered if Holland, or "Oliver X.," published regularly in such places; whether, after the ambition of his early twenties, he had a career at all. When Chatwin had known him—and he'd known him only slightly—he had been one of a number of young "artists" attached ambiguously to the University of Chicago. He had never distinguished himself in any way that Chatwin could recall, except by being so persistent in his overtures, so shyly obtrusive: always asking Chatwin to "glance through" something he'd written, always inviting "candid criticism." He was unfailingly polite, soft-spoken. "I know you're busy," he would say, fixing his moist dark eyes on Chatwin's, "but if you could just glance through this. . . . I'm not in any hurry to have it back." Was he the one, Chatwin tried to remember, with the pale freckled skin?—red curly hair, parted neatly on the left side of his head; a high rapid voice; an air of perpetual embarrassment. It was rumored that Oliver Holland's family was wealthy, but that had not disposed Chatwin in his favor. He was a nuisance, a burr, childlike in his very audacity, the sort of weak personality who assumes, even demands, that strong people cater to him, make a fuss over him. His head was too large for his narrow sloping shoulders, Chatwin remembered. His manner was too antic, too busy. He affected old clothes, shabby costumes, but certain of his accessories—a wristwatch, a pair of leather boots—were obviously expensive items: for some reason Chatwin, who had been genuinely poor, remembered this detail. A fraud, a hypocrite, he thought. A liar even then. He hounded Chatwin to have a drink with him and tell him "bluntly" what he thought of his latest play or batch of poems, but when Chatwin gave in, it seemed that he hardly listened. He nodded quickly, blinking, dipping his head, smiling a chill measured smile. "He doesn't care in the slightest what I think," Chatwin once told Yvonne, more puzzled than irritated. "Then why does he bother you so often?" Yvonne asked. "And why do you give in?"

Chatwin said he didn't know.

"Are you afraid to antagonize him?" Yvonne asked.

Chatwin said he certainly was not: he scarcely gave Holland a thought.

Yvonne pressed the point, as she usually did; and they quarrelled; and the subject of Holland was lost. Now, twenty years later, trying to remember that contemptible little bastard, Chatwin felt a surge of renewed anger toward Yvonne as well. It had always been her strategy, not before their marriage but after, to attack him by alluding to secret weaknesses in his personality. Failings and deformities which were obvious to others but hidden from Chatwin himself. . . .

By the time he exited for Mt. Rose he had dislodged the bandage over his rash by scratching vigorously around its edges. The rash should have healed by now but it still itched; in fact it throbbed with itching.

Lately it seemed to have spread to Chatwin's right elbow, to his neck, even to his earlobes. He feared an infection of the inner ear. But the pimples remained small and hard, and didn't swell into pustules; it must have been a secondary rash, Chatwin thought, and probably not very important. He would never see a doctor for such a minor ailment.

In any case scratching gave him a queer stealthy pleasure, a childish pleasure—until of course his nails drew blood.

Chatwin's first surpise was Mt. Rose itself—a derelict, melancholy extension of Newark, populated mainly by blacks, with shabby rowhouses, vacant lots heaped in rubble, boarded-up stores, junked cars left on the street. As Mt. Rose Avenue continued westward the neighborhood began to improve. Chatwin drove for several miles before stopping at a gas station serviced by white men, so that he could ask directions to the street Oliver Holland lived on.

He was surprised too at Holland's apartment building. It was small and foursquare and resolutely nondescript: a decaying stucco many years old, buff-colored, streaked with soot. A single skinny tree grew at the curb, the street was scattered with debris. Why is he hiding out *here*, Chatwin wondered. He sat for a few minutes in the car, watching the building, feeling his excitement build. His impulse was to open his valise and take a sip of whiskey but he made no move to do so. He did take the valise with him, however.

The afternoon was aglow with a warm, slightly humid sunshine, a vague air of Sunday elation. Was it spring? Was it already April? As Chatwin entered the building he drew a deep shaky breath and consoled himself with the stoic observation—as he always did when one of his plays opened, when, literally, the first official performance began—that, once begun, a certain sequence of actions was already speeding toward its conclusion; one no longer had to worry about initiating it. Fate was a matter of simple momentum at this point.

On the street it was spring; inside the old apartment building it was still winter, smelling of damp and must, of chill, of dirt. Chatwin climbed two flights of stairs with the nervous eagerness of an athlete; the very strain in his leg muscles gave him pleasure. It took him no time at all to find 3–D, Holland's door, but he didn't ring the doorbell immediately. By now his heart was pounding and a cold film of perspiration had broken out on his face and torso. He was in a high pitch of excitement: he chose to call it excitement, not nerves, not apprehension. It was an old trick of the theatre, to translate fear into exhilaration.

He pressed the doorbell and heard an interior buzz, disturbingly abrasive. Holland would recognize him when he opened the door, he would probably try to close the door in his face, so Chatwin would have to act quickly; he'd have to force his way inside. (But what if someone was with Holland?—he hadn't thought of that possibility until now.)

The door was opened almost immediately, however, and the thin, drawn, stoop-shouldered man who opened it didn't recognize Chatwin; and, for an awkward dream-like moment Chatwin didn't recognize him. *This* person?—Oliver Holland?—"Oliver X."?

Stammering slightly, not knowing quite what he said, Chatwin pushed his way into the apartment and shut the door behind him. He told the astonished man—it *was* Oliver Holland, much altered—that he'd come to speak with him about a certain manuscript, though he might have said—his words came in a rush, his voice shook—that he had come to deliver a certain manuscript. He made a gesture with the valise as if to hand it to Holland, but the gesture turned clumsy and rough; he actually shoved at Holland's thin chest, forcing him back.

"Don't you know me?—don't you recognize me?" Chatwin demanded breathlessly. The cubbyhole of a foyer was poorly lighted, he nudged Holland into the next room where they could see each other better. "You *are* 'Oliver X.,' aren't you?" he said in a voice heavy with scorn. "The autobiographer!—the pornographer! The *blackmailer.*"

At first Holland was too astonished to be frightened; then he recognized Chatwin, or grasped his identity; and a look of insipid terror, of virtual idiocy, overcame him. He raised both hands as if to ward off a blow. He stumbled backward against the edge of a table. Chatwin thought: Am I frightening him to death? What if I frighten him to death?

His own pulse was racing and exhilarated, his body felt radiant. He was saying in triumph: "Now you know who I am, don't you?—now you remember—the man you've slandered, you've been victimizing—the man you've been writing filthy lies about for months—"

They were in a shabby living room, hemmed in by oversized furniture, bookcases, an old-fashioned spinet piano with its keyboard closed, an oval dining room table at which evidently Holland had been working—a portable typewriter was set up at one end near the window, books and papers were scattered about, ceramic mugs, dirty plates and saucers, forks. Though the outside air was fresh and mild the window hadn't been opened, probably hadn't been opened in months: Chatwin noticed that at once. The place smelled sour, damp, cold. The smell of mourning.

"You must have expected me sometime," Chatwin said, still breathing hard. "Aren't you going to invite me to sit down?"

The man's pale lips moved almost inaudibly. What was he saying?—he didn't know who Chatwin was, he was going to call the building superintendent, the police—Chatwin couldn't just break in on him like this—

"Certainly you've been expecting me," Chatwin interrupted. "This is part of the plan, isn't it? Blackmail—*you*!"

But *was* this frightened man Oliver Holland?—so pale, drawn, stoop-shouldered, balding, he might have been a decade older than Chatwin himself, and not a few years younger. Yet the eyes were recognizable—moist, dark, slightly protuberant—and the pug nose, the prim little chin. Even the whining edge to his voice, his timid defiance. "I don't know anything about blackmail," he said. "I don't even know who you are. . . ."

"Certainly you know me," Chatwin said, shaking the valise at him, hearing his voice rise dangerously, "—I'm the 'C' of your memoir. Don't play dumb, don't play innocent. You must have known I would find out about it."

"I don't know what you . . ."

"Don't be ridiculous," Chatwin said angrily. "I'm not leaving until we've talked this through—until you know the seriousness of what you've done. Sit down. And stop staring at me like that, I'm not going to hurt you." Chatwin smiled at him, baring his big teeth. "Did you think I came here to hurt you?"

Holland was mumbling something vague and incoherent. He hadn't anything to say to Chatwin, he didn't have any idea what Chatwin was talking about. He was expecting another visitor shortly. He didn't have time for this. . . . His voice trailed off into silence.

With a show of impatience Chatwin let the valise fall on the table. He unzipped it as Holland cringed, he drew out a copy of the manuscript, slapped it about, spoke of its filth and malice, its sheer disgusting *fictitiousness,* every nuance, every exchange of dialogue, every "fact." Why had Holland slandered him? Why had he victimized *him*? It was enough to know that such homosexual filth had been written, so to speak, in his honor; but that Holland had had the temerity to send it around to magazines, to the offices of people who were acquainted with Chatwin, who would circulate it even further, and talk of it, and—

Though Chatwin was very angry he noted how Holland was looking furtively around, how he wasn't entirely *listening*—the very Oliver Holland of twenty years ago. He must have been calculating a way to push past Chatwin and escape, though Chatwin weighed at least thirty pounds more than he did, and was in much better condition. He could run past him and out into the corridor, shouting for help. He could lock himself in another room and telephone the police. Chatwin told him to sit down. "I'm not exactly *armed,* am I," he said in a voice heavy with sarcasm.

Holland repeated feebly that he hadn't anything to say to Chatwin, he was expecting another visitor. His freckles had evidently bleached out with the passage of years, or with the sudden force of his terror. A two- or three-day growth of beard, sandy-red, graying, gave his boyish face a dissolute look. "You are—you *are* going to hurt me," he whispered.

"Am I?" Chatwin said.

Holland sat heavily in one of the dining room chairs as if his knees had given out. Sunshine, slanting through a part-raised venetian blind, was unsparing with what remained of his old vanity: his skin was puffy, sallow, marked with premature wrinkles and creases, virtual dents in the flesh. His eyes were threaded with blood. He had the air of a convalescent—the apartment smelled of sickness, unwashed linen, dust. Staring at him, Chatwin felt a moment's vertigo: it was a shock to see Oliver Holland, who had always been so young, suddenly and irrevocably middle-aged.

"What in Christ's name has happened to you. . . ?" Chatwin asked.

Afterward Chatwin was to remember the visit, that visit of many hours, as dream-like, hallucinatory, distended in time. To ease the tension between them Chatwin drew out the bottle of Scotch with a mock-ceremonial flourish and insisted that Holland join him in a drink. ("I don't ordinarily drink at this hour," Holland said faintly. Though he was still badly frightened he spoke with his old prissiness, a hint of his old superiority.)

At first, however, what he had to say to Chatwin was barely coherent. He began a defense of some kind—he hadn't been well, a mysterious attack of the flu, protracted for weeks—hadn't been able to meet his classes—couldn't depend upon any friends (the word "friends" was uttered with particular venom) for help. Then he eyed Chatwin cautiously as if to gauge how much he could get away with, and said he had every right to "employ his imagination," as artists throughout history had done—as Chatwin himself had done. Before Chatwin could respond he said quickly, meekly: "I didn't think a person of your wealth and stature would care about such things. I really didn't think Lewis Chatwin would condescend to notice."

"Are you serious?" Chatwin said. "When you've libeled me?—concocted an utterly fictitious 'memoir' about me?"

Holland shifted anxiously in his chair and wiped at his nose. "How have I libeled you?" he asked quickly. "It hasn't been published, has it?—has any of it been published without my knowledge?"

He seemed genuinely frightened. Chatwin said that so far as he knew none of it had appeared—yet—in print; but why had Holland sent the material out if he didn't want it published? "Was it just straight blackmail all along?" Chatwin asked, trying to keep his voice steady.

"Blackmail! . . . that's ridiculous," Holland said. He shivered; he drew his bony shoulders up in a gesture of fastidious disdain that Chatwin remembered suddenly, from twenty years before. And it was in his old voice that he said: "I have a right, Mr. Chatwin, to exercise my imagination as I wish. 'Fragments of a Life' is a work of the imagination—it simply mimics the form of the memoir. It's an ingenious variation on an old theme. And you're crude enough to dismiss it as 'blackmail.' . . ."

Chatwin stared at him. Yes, that was the tone, that was the inimitable expression: half-chiding, reproachful, bemused: as if Chatwin knew full well that Holland was the superior talent, and that the world's estimate of their relative merit was contemptible. Chatwin remembered having thought back in Chicago, that Oliver Holland—that squeaking popinjay, that tenacious little boor—had the sort of faith in himself that Chatwin would have dearly loved to have in *himself*. From what wellspring of the soul did such confidence arise?—and was it necessarily unjustified?

He was speaking somewhat incoherently, charging Holland with having exploited his name; having led people to believe that the "Chatwin" in the memoir was him. "You haven't any right to exploit me like that," he said. "Of course it's blackmail—isn't it?"

Holland said quickly and irrelevantly that Chatwin had exploited many men and women in his career, after all; all writers did. And what right had he to force himself into a private residence as he had?—wasn't *that* a far clearer violation of the law?

Chatwin said thickly that he could bring charges of slander against him; and, if the material did show up in print, charges of libel. He had already spoken with an attorney, he said (though in fact he hadn't): a well-known New York attorney who handled such cases frequently. "He thought this case would be a particularly easy one to prosecute," Chatwin said. "After all, the memoir is totally fictitious and really, *really* very obscene. He said—"

Holland's expression was one of infantile alarm. He said, pleading: "But it *hasn't* been published, has it?—and it can't be published without my consent, can it?—don't they have to state their terms?—I mean editors—"

"But why otherwise did you send it out!" Chatwin shouted.

"My motive," Oliver Holland said, staring into his glass of Scotch, blinking slowly, ". . . was art."

Chatwin laughed incredulously. The conversation was mad, the very fact that he and his enemy were seated close together, sharing Chatwin's whiskey, was mad; yet it was taking place, and Chatwin had to confess that he was entirely absorbed. His excitement mounted sporadically; subsided; rose again; the encounter felt to him entirely *fated*, not a matter of his own volition at all. "You wrote that filthy thing solely to get attention for yourself, and to upset me," he said, "so that I'd be forced to deal with you. To pay you to withdraw it, to buy it from you. I suppose you really think that Lewis Chatwin is a man of 'wealth and stature'—!"

"You are," Holland said, raising his damp eyes to Chatwin's "You're famous."

"I am not *famous*."

"You're everything," Holland said passionately, "—and I'm nothing. *Not a thing has changed between us.*"

Chatwin looked away, embarrassed. He swallowed a large mouthful of Scotch and the taste was warm and consoling, and immediately strengthening.

Curious, that Oliver Holland couldn't afford a better apartment. This was a depressing place—indeed, a place for mourning. Chatwin noted that the comely little spinet piano had lost its polished sheen, and was piled high with books and magazines and old newspapers; the gigantic mahogany table—no doubt a family heirloom—was badly scuffed; the lampshades were discolored with dust; a faded needlepoint cushion lay on the floor. The old Oriental carpet was worn thin and smelled frankly of dirt. In a rococo-framed mirror on a nearby wall his and Holland's pallid reflections, diluted by sunshine, were caught in watery suspension. Chatwin said half-angrily that he'd thought Holland's family was wealthy: what had happened?

Holland shrugged his shoulders. "They were," he said sullenly, raising his glass to drink, "—for a while."

Chatwin considered his blackmailer—his persecutor. It was a novel situation, this, in which he could stare boldly and openly and arrogantly at another human being without fear of reprisal. In the ordinary course of events, after all, such behavior was forbidden; except perhaps to very young children or to the mentally defective. He and Oliver Holland, sequestered away in this room, alone together, and secretly. . . . It was an awkward scene, certainly. Yet exhilarating. The sort of thing, Chatwin thought, that could only be lived in the flesh—not mimicked on stage.

Chatwin said in a slightly accusing voice: "Yes, back in Chicago you had the reputation of being 'rich.' It was the only sort of reputation you did have. —Not that it meant anything to me."

"Of course not," Holland said. He sipped at his drink, grimaced, fought back a cough. He gave the impression of drinking Chatwin's Scotch only to placate him. "I realized that at the time."

"Nothing about you—nothing you did or said or hinted at—meant the slightest thing to me," Chatwin said.

"Of course not."

They sat for a while without speaking. Each was breathing audibly.

Finally Chatwin weakened and asked Holland why he was in

Mt. Rose. (It was a question he'd vowed not to ask because essentially he wasn't interested. He really had no interest.) But he asked, and Holland answered reluctantly that he was teaching Communication Arts at Seton Hall University. It wasn't a permanent position, he said; he wouldn't be staying in this dismal part of the world any longer than necessary. He had plans. . . . "Where were you before this? What has your life been like?" Chatwin asked curiously. Holland shrugged his shoulders again. He said that his life had been "inchoate" and "improvised" since the Chicago days. He had two, in fact two-and-a-half, graduate degrees. He'd done some free-lance journalism in Illinois that had come to very little; he'd spent a few years in Italy, and *that* had come to very little. Before Seton Hall he had taught for six years at San Francisco State until the university's budget was cut drastically and his entire program had been dissolved. . . . "I've always been an expendable person," he said with a childish smirk. "But of course you knew that."

Chatwin said impatiently that he didn't *know* anything about Holland, basically. Because he had never formed an opinion about him; he had never given him any thought.

"Of course not," Holland said with the same smirk.

"So you're hard pressed for money," Chatwin said. "And 'Lewis Chatwin' was the only person you could think of to blackmail. Right?"

Holland stared at him as if Chatwin had said something obscene. "I'm not that kind of person," he whispered. "I'd never stoop to anything so low as blackmail."

"But you have."

"I have *not*."

Chatwin tried not to become overly excited. It was bad for his nerves, maybe bad for his heart. Sometimes he was wakened in the middle of the night convinced that his heart had lurched and stopped beating. . . . But he couldn't stop himself from slapping the tattered manuscript against the edge of the table again, so violently that Holland cringed. "Do you want me to read some of this filth aloud?" he asked. "Are you provoking me?"

Holland made a show of pressing his fingertips against his ears. "Please stop," he said. "*Please*. You know very well that I have the right to compose anything I wish. It's my Constitutional right. 'The Spirit moveth where it will.' . . ."

"But you've concocted a fantasy," Chatwin said, "—a repulsive 'history'—in which I'm a principal character. You're trading on my name and reputation—you're exploiting me."

"How can you identify with *my* Chatwin?" Holland asked. His voice rose suddenly; his eyes had acquired an alarming brightness. "He's mine. I created him. I labored over him week after week—month after month. *I gave birth to him.* And now you burst in here and claim him and make threats and disrupt the quiet of my Sunday!—I think you're mad." He took another swallow of his drink and set the glass down hard. His voice trembled with the audacity of his words. "Do you really imagine you are my 'Chatwin'?—*you*? You flatter yourself!"

Chatwin said: "Don't provoke me, Holland. I only came to talk. I thought we might talk. In a civilized fashion. I thought we might come to some sort of agreement. . . ." Several of the manuscript pages had come loose and wafted to the floor, but Chatwin made no effort to retrieve them.

"Yes, you flatter yourself—you aren't 'Chatwin' *and you never were*," Holland said excitedly. "And you're spiteful!—envious! So you come here and intrude upon my privacy and talk of blackmail!—you, who've exploited so many people in your lifetime, you've forgotten most of them. I've been following your career closely, Chatwin, since we were friends in Chicago, and I've noted from time to time a certain character obviously based upon *me*—or, rather, upon your crude idea of me. (Of course you never knew me at all: I'm hardly an open book.) An object of pathos, an object of contempt—a peripheral sort of character—droll and 'queer'—drawing the superior laughter of the audience. I suppose you imagined I wouldn't guess who it was? As if you could exploit Oliver Holland without any consequences—!"

Chatwin protested: this really was absurd. He had never modelled any character in any of his plays on Oliver Holland; he'd never given him so much as a thought in twenty years. It might be said that Chatwin had based two or three of his strongest female characters on women he had known, but even these were composite portraits, hardly taken directly from life. But when he denied Holland's charge his voice sounded harsh and unconvincing, a bully's voice. "Why should I have written about you," he said, "—I hardly knew you in Chicago, I did my best to avoid you. You know very well—"

"Well—now *you* know," Holland said. "You know my power."

"All this is a strategem to disguise the fact that you want money from me," Chatwin said thickly. "Money or—or something. That—"

"Blackmail!—blackmail!" Holland cried, springing from his chair, flailing his arms about. "You're the one who keeps speaking of blackmail, not me! Please, Mr. Chatwin, I want only to write—to write as I please—to give my imagination a free rein. That's my privilege. That's anyone's privilege. You can't censor me despite your fame and power, you can't destroy my imagination. If I create a character named 'Lew Chatwin' that's my privilege—who can stop me? You'll have to kill me to stop me! Why, 'Oliver X.' is a fictitious creation as well. They are both extraordinary creations—utterly convincing—dozens of friends and colleagues have told me so. And several editors. There was an especially perceptive note from *Harper's*—most flattering. But of course the magazines are too cowardly to publish a work of such strength and audacity, despite the acknowledged excellence of the prose. What do they care for literary excellence, they're only terrified of being sued!—because they know *you*, they know how vindictive you would be. So it's a reverse sort of blackmail," Holland said bitterly. "You'd suck me dry if you could. You'd destroy me if you could."

Holland was pacing nervously about, still swinging his arms. Chatwin got slowly to his feet. The liquor had slightly dulled his reflexes but he had to be ready for a sudden move on Holland's part: he might have been getting up his courage, planning to rush Chatwin and attack him; or to run out of the room and barricade himself somewhere. It crossed Chatwin's mind that the man probably had a pistol in his bedroom; he was the type, the paranoid fussy cowardly type, to keep a gun. For self-protection, he'd say.

He noticed that Holland's feet were bare. White, bony, angular, with long toes. Very white. Dead white.

Holland was ranting, half-sobbing, accusing Chatwin of wanting to destroy him; boasting of his own talent; boasting of his "expert knowledge" of First Amendment law; threatening to sue Chatwin himself "if driven to it." Chatwin couldn't follow every word—the man spoke too fast—not very coherently. When he tried to interrupt, to remind Holland that he'd driven all the way from Manhattan so that they could talk this through in a civilized fashion, Holland shouted at him to stop: to please stop: his nerves couldn't take any more.

Both men fell silent. Chatwin could hear Holland's panting

breath—or was it his own? Somewhere in the apartment building a baby was crying; a telephone or a doorbell rang and rang, unanswered. The world was still *there*. . . . This struck Chatwin as a remarkable fact but he had no time to consider it.

He cleared his throat. He began to speak. He wanted Holland to admit that he'd done this all for money, simply to bring him to his knees—

Holland interrupted with another cry of anguish. His face was flushed and mottled, his eyes swam with tears. "That's a lie," he said. "And you know it. We both know it. You exploited my love for you long ago—you mocked me—I don't even mean in your plays—I mean in *life*. You didn't care about me. You didn't *know* me. You were everything and I was nothing and—"

"You're insane," Chatwin said, feeling his heart lurch. "You're inventing all of this. . . ."

"You mocked my love, my idiotic adoration," Holland said, his voice rising dangerously. "I didn't exist for you—you and whatever woman you were currently living with—'in love with'—I was invisible—a figure of contempt and pity. You were everything and I was nothing and you didn't *care*."

"That's ridiculous—"

"You didn't then and you don't now and *nothing has changed*."

"Stop it, you're hysterical—"

"*Nothing has changed and my life is over*."

Chatwin thought, panicked: He's inventing all this because he doesn't want to be hurt. And I don't want to hurt him.

He waited until Holland calmed down. Then he said: "Look. We can come to terms. We can agree on a price. But please don't provoke me any further."

It was six-thirty, or seven: the bottle was empty: the light had gradually dimmed so that Chatwin could barely make out Holland's features.

He was sitting with the opened valise on his knees, "Fragments of a Life" resting on top. Scratching half-consciously at his arm, poking his smallest finger in his ear to scratch it vigorously inside, Chatwin had forced Holland to listen to several of the more loathsome passages from the memoir: until Holland himself pleaded with him to stop.

Liquor rarely had any effect upon Chatwin. But poor Oliver Holland, sickly skinny Holland—*he* could barely hold his head up by this time and his words were slurred. Once or twice he had begged Chatwin to let him leave the room—he was about to be sick to his stomach—but Chatwin had called his bluff and forbidden him to move from his chair. And nothing had happened.

Now he pleaded to be "released."

His breath was audible. He might have been crying softly.

"You can't just keep me here like this," he whispered. "You don't say anything and you don't *do* anything and . . ."

"What would you like me to do?" Chatwin asked.

Chatwin regarded Holland—the man's vague shadowy cringing form—with a genial sort of contempt. He knew his enemy, he'd known him from the old days. They had recognized each other on sight. "What would you like me to do . . . ?" Chatwin asked quietly.

"But I don't have any price," said Holland. "I'm not a blackmailer."

Chatwin was in no hurry. He had all night if necessary. He had forever. By degrees the room grew darker but no one dared move to switch on a light, no one dared move at all.

STATEMENT

CAROL JANE BANGS

Because your pity didn't show
the first time you whispered my name,
because you brought food
when I was hungry,
and came to me with your thirst,
because your memories opened into fields
where I lived my alternate pasts,
because you showed me stones
to cross the sullen water,
taught me the names of things,
helped me find what mattered,
because you let me sink under you
until my breath almost stopped
and we found each other, rising up,
coming out of ourselves,
because you let me want you utterly
even when you wanted nothing,
because at least once you have met me,
perfectly, without doubt,
I am content, now, to love you
although we both are different people,
you telling me how little you need.

OUR ROSES

JAMES WEIL

The white floribunda
stay fresh for days
on my desk, while the

red ramblers wilt
overnight. You'd say
they belong on the fence,

which they do. I'd say
the white endure, the
red endear—they do

that too. But I haven't
asked you, and you
haven't asked me either.

It may be hard
persuading people this
actually happened.

MADONNA WITH CAT

CATHERINE PETROSKI

MADONNA WITH CAT, circa 1980
City Wilderness School, Artist Unknown

Mixed media

This depiction of the solitary spirit seeking refuge in the small pleasures of life occupies a central place in late 20th century American painting. The artist's ironic use of the madonna-and-child motif of Renaissance art typifies the School's sardonic view of the plight of contemporary man/woman.

(On loan from an anonymous private collector.)

Do you see the picture, hanging on the wall? Notice as well the walls themselves, the room, the ambience, the milieu: white on white, light from a pair of skylights, the floor a natural light oak. Study the picture with thought and care: it is a woman, a madonna with cat, Caucasian with Abyssinian.

Who is the woman? Perhaps one may only *begin* to describe her, place her within certain categories, seek the coincidence of sets, determine a context. She is a middle-class American woman. We can tell that much by her hair style, her makeup, her surroundings, and the way she holds her head. We can tell by her jewelry, by her wedding ring, by the age of the paint, which is not considerable. The internal evidence is overwhelming.

Let us then consider her beauty, or lack of it. Her age, or lack of it. What would you guess? Thirty? Forty? Who can tell? Even by indefinition, the artist defines, states: the purpose of much effort in this culture is to disguise such facts as age, and, being the product of a highly successful technological society, the artifact disguises the fact. Therefore, to the casual viewer—and can there be any other kind?—she is ageless. Now that she has become a painting, she once and for all transcends time. Her skin appears to glow (do you notice?) in the manner of the Sienese masters. The light falls on her garment (may I point out?) in the manner of the Flemish. And yet, the uncompromising expression in her eyes remains vulnerable, a quality which marks this woman as a product of her time, the age of technology. What do the eyes say? Is their message our correlative of the Mona Lisa's smile?

Should you look around the gallery, you may not be struck by any relationship between this work and others. Yet careful study will reward the museum-goer with insights linking this work, say, to that of Urbanoff's *Small Man, Large Lawnmower,* or Ciompi's *Tuning of the Executive Quartet,* or even Griffith's *Let Us Now Take the Children to the Zoo. Madonna with Cat* may be viewed as a culmination, though of what, perhaps we are too close, chronologically, to say.

Some among us have noticed that paradoxically, the painter has chosen anonymity. The fact that the artist chooses to remain unknown is something with which we may identify, but which we must not misinterpret. Some might claim it is thus to protect the identity of the subject, for notoriety can bring discomfort. We can be sure that this is a woman who would not enjoy coming face-to-face with herself in the market check-out on certain tabloid covers.

The painter says to us: What time could be less private, less anonymous than our own?

The painter says to us: I control what you know.

We say to the painter: Granted, but make it interesting.

CATALOG OF ATTRIBUTES

Hair: very nearly black, cut in short, blow-dry style. Casual. Note the artist's use of irony.

Eyes: two. Apparently alert, wide-set. Eschews heavy use of kohl, preferring instead persistent scrubbing, the open-eyed look. Mascara or good natural lashes. Hazel, irregularly colored: flecks of blue and amber. Possibly kind.

Skin: clear, taut. Good genes and/or expensive cream. Few worries, as confirmed by natural lack of gray; extremely smooth forehead raises concomitant possibility of few thoughts. A lucky woman, some would say.

Chin: present. Firm, held up, bespeaking determination, though to what end, no one knows.

Teeth: thirty. Extraordinarily straight and brilliant in their whiteness, perhaps another of the artist's concessions to overstatement. In themselves, a small miracle. [Not discernible to the naked eye, however: seven fillings, one crown, one root-canal.]

Expression, demeanor: a clear sense of presence, a patent smile, yet something in the eyes belies this placid exterior.

Regardez, mesdames et messieurs. Study the background here, and as you do, keep in mind the misty mountains of da Vinci. This is no Italian plain; this is Vermont. These small hills are packed close together, densely wooded with pine and birch and larch. Mark especially that the season is summer; the greens are deep. Judging by the golden light, the time of day is late afternoon, and let us say this is August. Remember that what we say doesn't change any of the facts, which are, to us, unknowable; we only speak of them, pretend to know them, because it comforts us.

Let us, then, try to imagine what has just happened, what has brought the real-life woman and the cat she holds to the point at which she is here captured for us. The light, as I have said, wanes, rosy and golden, departing as only sweet summer afternoons can. The perspective of the background, we should note, is oddly aerial, in the manner of certain Brueghels.

Let us further imagine that harpsichord music of the early 18th century fills the air, skipping about with its turns and grace-notes, suggesting a dance, which it may well originally have been. Let us suppose that the woman and her husband have just come downstairs from the bedroom where they make love to no avail, whether by choice or fate we cannot know.

And let us imagine further still that the afternoon, for all its color, has grown cool, and a fireplace full of fragrant apple boughs has just been lit, though the madonna herself prefers to stay outdoors on the porch of the house she has known since childhood.

Let us say that the first summer she can remember here was the summer when she was five: the house has not changed measurably since then, nor did it change very much in the preceding decades since the madonna's great-grandfather, a roller-skate baron, first bought the place to retreat from his eight children in the city. Let us further suggest that this woman is not one accustomed to want, yet her life now is consumed by a particular lack.

Perhaps of that we should not speak.

Let us instead study the cat.

To do so, indeed, is only an exercise in reciprocity. The cat, certain academicians have suggested, is perhaps the true center of this work. The cat, it seems certain, knows a great deal, more than the madonna, probably more than the artist, possibly more than anyone. There are orders of knowledge. The cat appears to know something significant about time, and, one must admit, there is little else to learn if one knows about time. The cat regards us from the madonna's circling arms. Regards us with a gaze knowledgeable and disinterested and superior. Regards not the painter, but the space in which the painter works: the movements of his arms, his pacing back and forth, his drinking from a can of Sprite. Regards the can with ears forward, catching the sounds of H_2O bubbles exploding inside the aluminum cylinder. Regards the window behind the painter, the trees behind the window, the lake behind the trees, the clouds behind the lake, the sky behind the clouds. Possibly regards something beyond that, seeing as dogs can hear.

There is no adoration in the visage of the cat, alas; the myth is shattered. He looks outward, not upward, knowing that if this madonna doesn't feed him, another will.

What were those summers like? Or is one summer ever any different from another? Is that the solace that summer offers, sameness? But look, the shadows of sleeplessness draw together beneath her eyes, the lonely contemplation of time.

Compare the cat.

Did those summers contain cats, also? Let us imagine a family album, kept at the house in Vermont for nearly a century, in which the roller-skate tycoon and his children, his grandchildren and his great-grandchildren are all recorded at the height of their summer negligence. Braids, knickers, and Buster Browns. Bloomers and middies and tank suits and campshirts. Sweaters, windbreakers, Levis.

Topsiders, flip-flops, sneakers, march on! Through these pictures roams a population of absurd devoted dogs and furtive cats: barking, wagging, guarding, fawning, begging; mesmerizing, condescending, playing children to these children. The dogs came along from the city, but from whence came these cats, and where did they go in September?

The cats, she might remember, came from nowhere and would not even ask to belong, to be permanent.

Let us know with the woman and her fancy permanent cat what it was about those cold nights (did she sneak a cat into her August bed?) and warm afternoons (did she ask a cat for tea and cakes?) those years ago in Vermont that made everything now possible, that forever after changed everything. Let us see in this painting the essence of the non-figurative and the anti-abstract. Let us know with touch and sound, smell, taste, and sight what this madonna, whose infant savior is a cat, is and has been—let us take it all in, every bit, instantly!

On one of the gallery's leather tufted benches sit two people. A man, about sixty-five, and a young woman of about twenty. Father and daughter, perhaps? The difference in ages is perhaps a bit too great for that to be the case. A roue up to no good with his Lolita?

"My sweet," the man begins.

"Professor, I can't."

"Hear me out, child. This motif you note—this appearance in human portraiture of a nonhuman animate creature—as in certain 18th-century German and Austrian court paintings—wherein favorite spaniels made regular appearances—the execution of which being generally superior to that of their human masters—perhaps it is worth some serious consideration. My love—my light—are you capable—at this point in your career—of realizing the potential of your perceptions? Come with me to my dusty study—and I will acquaint you—sweet child—with your need for a mentor—the wise and steady guiding hand you require to actualize what you have intuited here—believe me—dear child . . ."

Suddenly through the gallery door comes a videotape crew. Lights cables, cameras, and a staff of people to tell people not to get in the way of art. A recorded voice guides and inspires the taping crew—the commentary is already in the can. Richard Burton intones: "Before we leave the gallery, ladies and gentlemen, let us pause for a final moment, let us bow our heads in silent homage to the heart of the artist, of the madonna, and of the cat. Let us exercise our faith, which will teach us to know."

The lights go on. Show time. We turn our eyes away, having perhaps seen more than we should, having heard enough, or perhaps too much.

So alone we are back to the work itself.

Enough of loneliness and frustration, enough of beauty and its place on the time continuum, enough of what we do not know and never shall.

We disregard the surroundings, though they clamor to be noticed.

We disregard our fellow viewers, though they make absurd demands on our awareness.

We disregard the time in which the artist works, the fact that he draws special attention to himself by his posture of seclusion, the frame, the lighting, the tricks of techniques and, in certain regards, the lack of technique.

We disregard everything except the madonna and the look in her eyes, the look in the cat's eyes, and the moment at which we all look at each other, for that is the magic. That is the still point, and the still point is the point. What the madonna's lacks or failings are, what she has acquired, what she desires are for the moment of apprehension irrelevant. What the madonna is, here, is all that matters.

And seeing her, each time we ask again, what *is* this madonna and what this cat?

TWO POEMS ON DESIRE

BRIAN SWANN

"... all alone, all free, all unique."—Rinzai

1.

Eye wakened—
        flip of a leaf
                on the sapling elm.

Came back the years I felt
        there was nothing in the world:
                couldn't see what there was.

I looked to concepts,
        ignoring the round.
                Nothing I could see shocked

the world into being itself,
        in such a place and
                nowhere else. Now, however,

I am a light catching
        what I throw. What I take
                is nothing. Yet ten years

I've been looking out this
same window & I've never seen
the same things twice.

But I am not free.
I desire. So again
I got out, falling around

in snow—to awaken without
fixing anywhere. Not leaf.
Not tree. The perfection

of the snow stretching
into sky, jumping
the valley.

The valley is over my head.
I disappear at the waist.
The rest still looks about.

2.

Ate lentils. Fried the cakes
in sesame oil. Rain, a ripened lens,
blocks windows, glazes snow and

repels smoke. Young pines hoop where rain
tightens to ice. Blue of glass is
never so blue, brown so brown,

translucence never so dimensional, never
so full of tracks & shadows. If only
the light held another light,

not intensity but a narrowing
that probes as you dream: a contract
that would hold as places

shift, as sky's grit lies about
        slicking wild-cleared slabs so you
                can't move on, though

the river can, gliding its ice up the bank,
        shattered panes tossing light
                in all directions, grinding out

the noise of an express ringing tracks
        miles ahead, the tide going out,
                air reaching under ice to blossom

white & alveolar, whole trees breathing,
        raw space pushing in and up,
                emptiness clawing out

desire.

THREE POEMS

BARENT GJELSNESS

DAEDALUS IN THE DESERT

"The sun burns bright orange,
Harsh, overhead.
What disguise
Suits me today?
Which mask is best?
The Minotaur's?

But as I start
To put it on,
A flock of crows
Attacks my face and eyes,
Their wings and cries
Beating at my ears.
I shield my head
With my forearms,
Which bleed
From the work of their beaks.
They drive me to my knees.
I stutter and shake.
Shadows disappear,
And all relief.
Then the white

Desert stones
Begin to speak.
Who are you,
They say in chorus,
To presume
To take up
This sacred face?
By whose permission
Do you dare
Become The Beast
So secretly born
Whose power is here
Despite your hideous
Complacency, which is
Harder than we.
Only to us is it given
To sing the Minotaur's song.
Mortals like you can never
Know him, know him, know him . . ."

I answer in anger,
And in fear.
I bellow.
The crows scatter.

I begin to sing.
My song hovers brightly
Between darkness and darkness.
The desert's white light
Lifts it up.
All masks are mine,
All songs.
Whatever form I take
Becomes the sign
Of my design.
Whatever mortal longs
For immortality
Remembers me
And for my sake

His self will break
Set free
The spirit world, a sea
Inside him.

The souls of stones
Escape when they crack.
The souls of men
Escape when they lack
Nothing at all,
Are weightless,
Never fall.

Though there was no one
To hear me
But the stones,
I sang and walked
And sang again,
In the sun,
In the sun,
Not yet undone."

DAEDALUS AGAINST DAEDALUS

As I gave the wings to Icarus,
My son, my eyes were filled with tears.
It was so unlike me to give way
To feeling, like a woman:
So completely out of character.
I, of all people,
Who placed so much stock
In self-control, the stoic will,
(The purity of reason
Untainted by passion),
The steady flame which was
The only guarantee

Of the eternal
Contact with Apollo.

Well, I wept. I knew what would happen,
Knowing my son. In his ecstasy
He would vie with the winds,
With the sun itself. And he would die.
He would wheel and fall, like a spent
Star. I would find his feathers
Floating in the tidewash.
I would find him.
Slack, quiet body,
Too white, still limber,
Almost
As if he were asleep
After a long swim,
And would soon
Open his eyes, greet me
With his wicked grin.

DAEDALUS ON HIMSELF

Before I fled to Sicily from Crete
I left my votive offering
At Aphrodite's shrine:
A golden honeycomb
To help appease the gods.
I left it very near the place I pushed
My nephew Telos to his death.
I murdered him for reasons:
Because of jealousy,
Because I could ill afford
A rival so effortlessly
Skilled, so apt for power,
And so ambitious,
And because of his open
Incest with my mother.

Telos had invented
The saw in iron,
Merely from noticing
The white spine of a small
Fish's skeleton.
The potter's wheel
Was also his idea.
And the circle-drawing
Compass of many uses.

Of his lascivious
Amusements with my mother
I will say only this:
They were too much
Even for me, for whom
Blasphemy is easy.
Their serpentine
Intertwinings were
The one unnatural act
I could not forgive.
Therefore I killed him,
Rushed down from the sun-
Drenched heights of the Acropolis,
And shoved his shattered
Puppet's body into a sack.
I was seen by citizens
Just after that, and said
That I was picking up
A snake's remains
As the law required.
(Which was half-true.
Telos was half-snake,
An Erechtheid.
Between his toes and fingers,
Under his trim beard
And shadowy jawline,
There were tiny scales.
I know. I have them too.)

My disguise
As a dutiful
Street cleaner
Might have been believed,
But bloodstains on the sack
Gave me away.
It has ever been so:
Bad luck is seldom random.
It stalks the skilled
No less relentlessly
Than it does the simple
Victim in his maze,
Bungler in his daze.

I fled before my trial could occur.

I continued to create.
For young Peleus
I forged a golden sword
And charged it with my power,
So that he could never
Lose in war, nor fail
In any hunt for game,
His favorite bear,
Deer, or boar.
And though the Centaurs
Stole it from him cynically,
Their own king Cheiron
Gave it back again,
So binding was its magic.

For fair-haired Ariadne
I made a dancing floor;
For Apollo, a temple
With golden rooftops;
For Icarus, a sturdy cradle
And the wings you know.

For humankind, I made
The robot and the wheel.
The cleanest distillations
Of my mind
I gave to amateurs,
Who would misuse them.
Ludicrous fools
Unable to comprehend
The beauty of simplicity
Would make of it a sterile
Artificial mind,
Complex and stupid,
But subtle enough
To give them the illusion
That it was their creation,
Under their control.
The vanity of novices!
Their plodding variations
On the pure children
Of my teeming brain
Would have concerned me more,
Had I been clairvoyant.

I made
The logical extensions
Of my own lucidity.
What others made of them
Was no affair of mine.

As architect for Sicily
I made the public buildings,
Private homes, estates
Lavish as the plans
For my own future.
For Cocalus' daughter
I made some lovely toys.

Then I murdered sly Minos,
Fled Sicily for Sardinia,

And there lived out my life
Ever heavier with honors,
Celebrated
Into coiled old age,
Still creating
My secret combinations.
You can still see them.
They are called Daedaleia.

Shall I now
Drag in a moral for this tale?
Why not?
Make toys as well as temples.
Run when you must.
Settle when the time
Has ripened.
Keep your eyes open,
Your heart closed,
And your wits well honed.

THE POWER OF "NEGATIVE" THINKING

The "Grotesque" in the Modern World

ROBERT E. HELBLING

1. In the Grotto of the Grotesque

Some years ago, Bella Abzug, exasperated over some political shenanigans, exclaimed in frustration: "It makes you laugh, but it's not funny!" She may not have realized it, but her offhand remark cuts through a thicket of academic discourse and provides us with a deft formulation for the emotional impact of the grotesque, namely a mingling of fascination and revulsion. The experience of the grotesque is caused by something that shocks, even frightens us and yet strikes us as risible. Right at the outset, however, it must be noted that the grotesque is subject to a good deal of cultural and social conditioning, even to personal sensibilities, but as a concept denoting an emotional complex it has shown remarkable consistency over the years. No matter *what* produces the grotesque sensation, it is taken for granted *that* something does and in the appropriate instances elicits roughly the same response. *Esse est percipi!*

An Amazon Indian suddenly displaced into a modern operating room, with its tentacular gear and the noseless creatures manipulating it, might find the scene both terrifying and funny. Similarly, a Western "dude" witnessing the ritual dances and martial paraphernalia of an Amazon tribe may feel a few shivers of fright running down his back while politely trying to contain a spate of titters. It is especially the "comic" or mirthful element in the grotesque that is susceptible to cultural relativism, while there may exist archaic fears buried in the "collective unconscious" that are shared by all humanity and may be aroused by such things as snakes and skulls or the teeming life of a jungle. Monkeys are said to have an instinctive fear of snakes and skulls—something else that we hominoids may have in common. Sad to say, certain forms of physical freakishness in human beings, as displayed for instance in Victorian sideshows or portrayed with a thick palette in some films by Federico Fellini, may affect us as *inherently* fearful and ludicrous, therefore grotesque.

But a prolonged exposure to the strange and "weird" breeds familiarity: snakes may become pets, skulls an adornment on a paleontologist's desk. To the contemporary citizens of Paris, the gargoyles of Notre Dame are as comfortable as a pair of seasoned loafers and, of late, most of us have become jaded about the sartorial and cosmetic grotesqueries of Punk Rock stars and, for better or for worse, the glib "nukespeak" of nuclear deterrence alcoholics. Over the centuries and decades, cultural transformations, the eroding force of time, the dulling effect of the *déjà vu*, have obviously wrought marked changes in human susceptibilities to the grotesque.

The origins of our modern concept of the grotesque are harmless enough. Some fifteenth-century excavations in a huge *grotta* in Rome brought to light a series of fanciful murals decorating the Domus Aurea of Nero, the palace of Titus and others. This decorative style is characterized by a strange interweaving of plant, animal, human, and architectural forms, amounting in Santayana's placid phrase to a "rejection of the natural conditions of organization."[1] Natural physical realms disintegrated and were reassembled in a novel way to suit the whims and fancies of the artist—a horse with legs of leaves, a human head leering out of a tulip blossom, for instance. Familiar landmarks in the evolution of the "grotesque" are the paintings of Hieronymus Bosch and the two Brueghels, which, however, no longer serve mere decorative purposes. Their canvasses are often terrifying landscapes of anxieties, hallucinatory visions replete with infernal creatures composed of disparate elements, which make us shrink back in horror, though their incongruous shapes may elicit an amused chuckle. In fact, Brueghel the

Elder's paintings of the disquieting elements in human language—a series of visual portrayals of proverbs depicting a topsy-turvy world, both sinister and comical—suggest the lurking presence of satanic laughter on the satiric fringes of the grotesque.

The subsequent empirical history of the grotesque in art and literature fills volumes. But, absorbing as that history may be, more important to our understanding of the wayward artistic mode and its attendant emotional complex is the question after its psychological and mental wellsprings. Why the fascination with frightful-ludicrous aberrations, and how is it possible to experience—simultaneously!—such discrepant emotions as horror and mirth or fear and laughter? Here we open a Pandora's box, or more down to earth, a "can of worms." Fear by itself is rather easily aroused; not so fear *and* laughter. Therefore, the plethora of horror shows on TV and in the films that scares youthful or immature audiences right out of their Adidases! But what's funny about them?

A few theories with varying degrees of cogency and persuasiveness stand out. Hegel, forever sniffing out the hiding places of the world spirit, suggests that in grotesque distortions the *super*natural appears in the guise of the *un*natural.[2] Indeed, some Romantic art and literature in Germany suggests that grotesqueness is an inverted expression of the pure spirit, which manifests its profound dissatisfaction with the phenomenal world by wreaking havoc with it, much as airborne kitchen utensils and oozing walls may betray the vagaries of an addled poltergeist.

In our day, the heir to this ontological view is Wolfgang Kayser, who maintains that the grotesque originates in some cryptic, metempirical power which subverts and undermines the familiar by the uncanny and alien. For want of a better term, Kayser called this irruptive power simply the "It," turning Hegel's occasionally rambunctious "spirit" into a capitalized pronoun. What intrudes suddenly into the familiar, according to Kayser, ultimately remains incomprehensible, inexplicable, and impersonal. This theory, though rather tenuous, at least shows that in its grotesque accouterment the familiar world is never wholly absent but always on notice of possible discharge.

Kayser's theory may strike us as all too speculatively Germanic. As Poe was led to say: "If in many of my productions terror has been the thesis, I maintain that terror is not of Germany, but of the soul."[3] Following Poe's hint, we should perhaps rummage around in the grotto of our psyche rather than at the lunatic fringes of the cosmos to find the lair of the grotesque. In a world obsessed by psychoanalytic curiosity the switch was made easily enough. With a prestidigitator's alacrity, the ontological "It" became the psychological "id," the upper-case "I" a lower-case letter, as we descend from higher to lower regions.

There are admittedly primal, atavistic powers lurking in the psyche—dredged up by Freud, Jung, and their cohorts—associated either with the elemental life forces of Eros, but also with infantile aggressiveness, or even the destructive thrusts of Thanatos (the death instinct), which recurrently assail the frail structure of the ego, causing no mean fears in us. The mechanism by which the grotesque emerges serves the purpose of *disarming* such frightening, archetypal eruptions by infusing them with elements which under favorable circumstances elicit derisive laughter. The laughter is a defense mechanism, a temporary refuge from a psychological menace, perhaps also a desperate affirmation of "sanity," a manifestation, if you will, of the homoeostatic device built into the psychic apparatus. The laughter cannot be attributed to the conscious mind's deriving enjoyment from the discomfiture caused by the surprise visit of some *daemon absconditus.* It is rather a form of "whistling in the dark," which is hardly a masochistic thrill. We can summarize the mechanism with the slogan: "the daemonic made ludicrous,"[4] which is a form of exorcism.

The exorcist theory seems to work best when applied to distorted humanoid creatures—dirt freaks, bogeys, tricksters, what have you—that occur in the folktales or mythologies of most cultures. When applied to folklore, it might be called the "goose-bumps" theory, accounting as it does for mild rashes of fright soothed by therapeutic laughter. The theory is, however, loosely connected with serious scholarly investigations into the roots of folk festivals, carnivals, fairs, black masses (nowadays maybe rock festivals), when official culture and social structures were turned topsy-turvy—in the Middle Ages for instance, priests braying like asses throughout the mass and using excrement instead of incense during solemn service. The grotesque emerges, then, as a concept of liminality, showing society teetering between order and chaos, sense and non-sense. Not content with mere anthropological description, some critics attempt to reduce these manifestations to primitive psychological complexes, for example to Melanie Klein's theory of cannibalistic, infantile phantasies directed against the parents, hinged up in turn with derivative Freudian notions of Oedipal aggressiveness toward oppressive authority in general.

However, the more psychologically reductionist some of these theories are, the less they seem to come to grips with the grotesque in the contemporary world. Sensing this dilemma, William Van O'Connor in a seminal essay connects the grotesque with the tremendous social, political, and cultural dislocations that have occurred in our era, especially poignant in the South of the United States. These upheavals resonate in the individual psyche, cause a detachment from "reality," even a loss of vitality, and may breed frightening abnormalities. As a prime example, O'Connor cites Faulkner's *As I Lay Dying*: "the weird funeral journey, the rough box falling into the stream, Cash's riding on the box with his broken leg, the putrescent corpse, the belated struggle of Jewel and Arl for Addie's love"[5]—all the episodic material suggesting genuine human involvement and moral sensibility as patently missed opportunities. To what extent such episodes evoke defensive laughter in us may be a moot point.

2. The Power of "Negative" Thinking

The exorcist theory, centered as it is on defensive laughter as a buffer against atavistic fears, may prove inadequate in shedding light on the grotesque in the contemporary world. The history of the mode shows that successive generations have had to redefine the grotesque in terms of what they perceive as threats to their very own sense of essential humanity. Today, we might be well advised to look for the masked dangers of the grotesque, not in the penumbra of the psyche, but in the glare of a strangely distorted social and political world. And it is debatable whether its ludicrous side—dimly perceived or explicitly portrayed—serves the purpose of diminishing the horror and making a bad dream more bearable.

No doubt, a good portion of our film production, replete as it is with poltergeists, werewolves, resurrected Draculas and Frankensteins, caters to the infantile nightmares in the audience and the adult need for cash in the producers. And the nervous guffaws elicited by the crudities displayed in some of these films, as in

Friedkin's notorious *The Exorcist* of a few years ago, may attest to the defensive function of a certain type of laughter. But most of us either pay these creations the ultimate tribute of ignoring them or take them for what they are: momentary titillations. A more ominous note is struck, however, in the tawdry world of the bad trip, where Leary and his disciples have encountered daemons steeped in a grotesque ambiance:

> The visual forms appear like a confusing chaos of cheap, ugly dime-store objects, brassy, vulgar and useless. The person may become terrified at the prospect of being engulfed by them. The awesome sounds may be heard as hideous, clashing, oppressive, grating noises.[6]

But, undaunted, they claim that such hallucinations are necessary to an ultimately salutary ego-loss, way stations in a pharmaceutically induced inner journey to the sublime, a Romantic quest abetted by a dubitable chemical magic.

Compared with the grotesques in today's social and intellectual realms, the psychedelic exorcism of our private demons or the bugbears arising from archetypal fears within us seem like child's play. Symptomatically, the comic disarming of monstrous childhood fantasies, as in *The Muppet Show* or *Sesame Street*, in the ravenous cookie monster, for instance, has the opposite effect of its pedagogic intention as a warning against retrograde behavior: "I may be as ugly as culinary sin, but I'm really lovable." I wonder how many three-year-olds walk the streets, proudly exclaiming: "I'm a monster!"

Of late, even the fearful monsters of our infantile imagination projected into outer space in many a sci-fi movie have been dulcified. The interstellar drifters that congregate in some galactic bar in *Star Wars*, though no doubt an *outré* assembly of grotesque shapes, are just a rowdy bunch of humanoid desperadoes. In other films, the erstwhile monsters have become harbingers of supreme goodness—the evanescent creatures in *Close Encounters of the Third Kind*, the rubbery darling E.T., symbolizing our need for something better than we are and implicitly giving the lie to the chauvinistic belief that the human being in its classicist Greek shape, helped along by jogging and aerobic dancing, is the crown of creation (maybe children *are*, but not adults, as is amply made clear through the child's viewpoint in *E.T.*)! In these films, grotesque shapes have virtually become redemptive figures, in the sense of "showing the way" to moral goodness and personal responsibility, as in nineteenth-century fiction did Dostoevsky's Christ in the "Grand Inquisitor" episode.[7]

These highly profitable ventures may be seen as peripheral manifestations of the disquiet caused in us by the civilization we have created. But we can find a keener awareness of the grotesque deformations at the core of modern society in certain forms of serious art and literature. Stylistically, two major tendencies can be observed: one in which imaginative episodes abound, another where realistic happenings are portrayed with a cool, Kafkaesque matter-of-factness, causing as the psychologists used to say, a "displacement of affect" in the viewer or reader.

In the first category, one could mention Kurt Vonnegut, Jr., for instance his *Cat's Cradle* or *Slaughterhouse Five*. Aficionados of Donald Barthelme may wish to adduce him. But in his stories, "meanings" buzz around exasperatingly like pesky flies that are hard to swat, and some of Vonnegut's novels, for that matter, are full of narcissistic giggles about the difficult craft of writing modern fiction. Among many possible examples, Günter Grass's *The Tin Drum* stands out. It is an impressive literary achievement, contains an interesting mix of the psychological and sociological grotesque, and a few years ago was ingeniously transposed to the screen in Schlöndorff's remarkable film of the same name.

In a memorable opening scene (invented for the film), we see the infant-hero Oskar in his mother's womb, as he prepares, with furrowed brow, to make his exit in order to face a deranged world as well as his two fathers, one legal, the other biological. From thereon he lives a life of infantile aggressiveness (reminiscent of Melanie Klein's theory) or, as one critic puts it, "a life of Oedipal wishes [lived out] with almost excessive fulness."[8] For instance, he points an accusing finger at Jan, his natural father, suggesting that he is ignominiously using an innocent child as a cover for enemy bullets, and thereby helps pushing him over the edge of sanity to a grotesque death. Or, later on, he affixes on Mazerath, his legal guardian, a Nazi Party pin when the Russians swarm through the house. As one of the soldiers pumps a few bullets into Mazerath, who is trying to conceal the pin by gulping it, Oskar cavalierly squishes a louse between his fingers.

But these acts—as are Oskar's intentional fall from the stairs, which dwarfs him for life; his drumming; his glass-shattering with his high-pitched voice; his participation in the Duster's gang—are also acts of counteraggression against a society gone mad. Memorable the scene under Nazi-rostrum, where Oskar's drumming cuts up the rhythm of a marching band, sending the whole martial parade into an orgy of confusion; he listens to the sound of a different drummer. Memorable also the SA-man who cuts open dolls with his dagger and seems "disappointed each time that nothing but sawdust flowed from their limbs and bodies."[9] A classic scene of contemporary grotesque is the clinical description of the laughing horse's head hauled ashore from the brackish waters of a bay, its brain eaten out by eels, slimy creatures gnawing at the nerve center of a benign being, suggesting perhaps the disease festering at the very core of a helpless society.

Günter Grass's seemingly humorous portrayal of unalloyed horror is no mere comic disarming of an incipient threat. Certainly, he did not design his impish, subversive dwarf to elicit the kind of laughter that would afford his reader relief from the guilt and suspicion of having neutrally witnessed, tolerated, or even abetted Nazi—or for that matter, any other—fascistic aggression. Yet, in this morally and socially oriented grotesque, which I claim to be the most significant contemporary version of the old mode, there is apparent ambiguity, at least on the surface level of literary description.

Oskar, acting in anarchic isolation without a readily identifiable cause, seems ludicrous by the very ineffectuality of his enterprise within a larger historic context. On the face of it, his aggressive acts, especially the havoc he causes with his high-pitched, glass-shattering voice, appear as a futile, though daemonic, threat to the social order. But what order! Theoretically, one could of course say that in the morally informed grotesque either the oppressor or the oppressed, or for that matter both, may be either daemonic or ludicrous, or both, depending on the polemic aims of the portrayer.[10] In the case of Grass's *The Tin Drum* the intent is obvious: the ludicrously daemonic (the strutting Nazis) can best be fought by the daemonically ludicrous (the mischievous dwarf). The candor of a Candide, the simple-mindedness of a Simplizissimus, or the naiveté of a Soldier Schweik would not do.

The important point is: the clash between the two destructive systems in Grass's novel illustrates *par excellence* the making of the contemporary serious-minded grotesque. Through its artistic and stylistic means it mirrors the very nature of the thing it polemicizes, namely *the conspicuous absence of any reliable standards of moral reason.* Assuredly, Günter Grass is not striking a blow for the dubious values of most contemporary form of terrorism.

Our world is beset by all kinds of oppressive codes, political, social, religious, economic, ideological. But "code" does not necessarily mean "ethics." The Mafia has a code, too, the popular fascination with which proved to be such a rich lode of lucre for the producers of *The Godfather* films. The nihilist or anarchist that seemingly lurks in Oskar's soul is in reality a closet moralist. Before the seeds of a new moral sensibility can be sown, one must cut deep, upsetting furrows. Therein lies one of the positive powers of "negative" thinking! (A number of library boards across the country might be well advised to keep that in mind before they remove certain literary works from their shelves! Holding up the proverbial mirror to a grotesque world is not ipso facto a moral offense!) It may well be that even the "punks" that occasionally roam the streets of our cities are not merely promulgating new sartorial and cosmetic fashions. Like Günter Grass's Oskar, at least a few of them may be closet moralists in gaudy disguise, though I do not wish to acclaim them: they lack taste!

For a brief discussion of the second category of the contemporary social grotesque—the studied understatement of horrors—a good visual example is Nahum Tschaebasov's painting *Madonna and Child with Gasmasks,* done in 1938. It shows a Madonna with Child in a pose that reminds us of the sublimity of a Botticelli painting, forever trembling on the verge of Christian mystery. But they stare at us from behind the hollow eye sockets of ugly gasmasks. The technological "overlay" infuses the aura of the ethereal with an element of the ridiculous and horrific; the spirit gassed away, so to speak.

In literature, one of the best cases in point is the central episode in Curzio Malaparte's novel *The Skin.* The dried-out skin of a soldier neatly flattened by the caterpillars of a tank is used as a flag on the shovel of a jubilant partisan. The author describes the scene with apparent dispassionate, scientific, "objectivity":

The face had assumed a square shape, and the chest and stomach were splayed out at the sides in the form of a diamond. The outspread legs and the arms, which were a little apart from the torso, were like the trousers and sleeves of a newly pressed suit, stretched out on the ironing-board.

. . . .

[The partisan] walked with his head high, and on the end of his spade, like a flag, he carried that human skin, which flapped and fluttered in the wind exactly as a flag does.[11]

A human skin, nervously fluttering in the wind, hungry for life's animation, strikes us as more than a mere comic spoof and as something less than a dignified tragic character. Our emotions are probably kept in suspense between dismay and stealthy mirth. The unexpected utilitarian capacity of a human skin certainly takes us by surprise.

We can find another classic example in Joseph Heller's *Catch-22* of about twenty years ago, a novel which is consistently grotesque, most of its episodes marked by the intertwining of the comic and the horrific. No doubt, this novel is a milestone in contemporary fiction precisely on account of this quality. I am referring to Kid Sampson's being sliced in half by the propeller of a plane, an episode which Heller describes with surgical precision and surface amusement:

There was the briefest, softest test! filtering audibly through the shattering, overwhelming howl of the plane's engines, and then there was just Kid Sampson's two pale, skinny legs, still joined by strings somehow at the bloody truncated hips, standing stock-still on the raft for what seemed a full minute or two before they toppled over backward into the water finally with a faint, echoing splash and turned completely upside down so that only the grotesque toes and the plaster-white soles of Kid Sampson's feet remained in view.[12]

A last literary example of this "cold" grotesque, as some critics call it: Friedrich Dürrenmatt's play *Der Mitmacher* (best translated as "The Fellow-Traveler," but without Communist overtones), a pungent grotesque of contemporary society as a Mafialike network, in which everyone is an accomplice in one way or another. It centers on the figure of "Doc," a scientist and intellectual who against his better insight goes along with a corrupt system by putting at its disposal his newest invention: a viral action machine called a "necrodyaliser" that dissolves bodies into pure water. Again to the point, the language stands in grim contrast to the content: banal everyday phrases set against the sound of water flushing in the background. Deadly power games linguistically trivialized! The Kafkaesque dispassion of such "cold" grotesques may have a more lasting effect on us than, say, the searing rhetoric and ponderous theatricality of the macabre final scenes in Francis Coppola's film *Apocalypse Now*.

But we should be aware that we are not dealing in these instances with the blasé foolery and glib buffoonery known to us from gallows and deadpan humor or medical school jokes. These usually serve as a screen between our sensibilities and pervasive horrors and may cater to our frivolous need to be titillated by horror rather than to face it. How else explain the massive popularity of the *MASH* and even less distinguished TV series?

In the *MASH* program there is only the faintest echo of the grotesqueries that could be found in the initiatory movie, epitomized in its theme song whose lilting melody contrasted, Brechtian fashion, with the shocking lyrics "Suicide is painless." In the series, the melody can still be heard, but significantly the words have been left out: in comparison with the movie, the TV program is a shortcut to the excitement of war without the reality. In its dialogues, the continual quips, put-downs, the lightning gags, and even quicker Neil Simonesque punchlines create an entertaining atmosphere of cute frivolity, which was effectively parodied a few years ago in the teenage magazine *Mad*: In one panel a headless body is seen, kept alive by an intravenous tube extending into the thorax through the neck-stump. The following dialogue ensues:

—I don't see anything *funny* about all this suffering. This man was hit in the *leg!* Think that's *funny*?

—No.

—This man was hit in the chest! Think *that's* funny?

—No.

—And this man's *head*'s been blown off. . . .

—Now *that*'s funny!

The banal tone of the whole series is cleverly ridiculed in the next repartee:

—Oh! And *what*'s so funny about *that*?

—Just wait till he tries to comb his hair.[13]

It is manifestly difficult to be grotesque night after night! The witticisms of the series occasionally have the makings of black humor, though of a rather anodyne variety. This type of humor, along with some grotesqueries, is practiced, however, with lubricious abandon in the Monty Python productions, where it often slips over the edge of the merely funny into scurrility, licentious abuse, and blasphemy, with the avowed purpose of giving offense to the prudish while entertaining the more bohemian folk. The ribaldries of the performances often suffer from histrionic self-indulgence. Outrage at our deadly follies may become drowned in too much loony outrageousness, especially if one is half in love with one's own outrage, as I suspect the Monty Pythons occasionally are. Their loopy scenarios often tend to be more gross than funny, though some episodic material may have the underlying seriousness of the grotesque or the sting of black humor.

Black humor is probably still best embodied in the well-known Charles Addams cartoons which have enlivened the genteel pages of *The New Yorker* from the 1940s on. In comparison with the genuine grotesque, black humor has a rather sadistic tendency and its targets are usually more specific—conventional family and social attitudes monstrously travestied (parents endearingly watching their children chopping off dolls' heads with a guillotine, for instance). And witty captions or commentaries make it quite clear what or who the victims of the withering humor are.

A good example of a possible mix of the grotesque and black humor is that remarkable film *Dr. Strangelove* made about twenty years ago. Especially pungent is the final scene of the Texan pilot astride an atomic bomb, patriotically brandishing his ten-gallon hat as he zooms in on his target; a takeoff perhaps on the lurid secret that the bomb dropped on Hiroshima was adorned with the famous rear view of Betty Grable.[14] Earlier in the film, the spasmodic gestures and the leering smile of the eponymous hero provided a number of fine visual grotesqueries.

Black humor and the like may be spinoffs of the grotesque. If we are not too punctilious with our terms we may call these phenomena "grotescent." And if we are pontifical and wish to peer behind their facade of frivolousness and scurrility, we might say that their luxuriant growth in our time betrays a widespread sense of loss of value.

The point I wish to make, however, is that the apparent deadpan humor of the "cold" grotesque is no cheap thespian legerdemain or tomfoolery. It is rather the result of our realization that language, ever since the Holocaust and the Bomb, can no longer express the terrors we have wrought without falling prey to the hyperbole of justifiable hysteria or, worse, the unctuousness of didactic preachments. This is one of the meanings of Friedrich Dürrenmatt's statement in his *Problems of the Theatre,* one of the more incisive dramaturgic manifestos written in our day: "Our world has led to the grotesque as well as to the atom bomb, and so it is a world like that of Hieronymus Bosch whose apocalyptic paintings are also grotesque."[15]

Our everyday language imitates spontaneously, without our being much aware of it, the conscious stance of the writer of "cold" grotesques. We only have to listen to the language in our press and other media to get the point: there is a good deal of *unintentional* grotesque there, depending of course on our threshold of linguistic sensibility.

A few months ago, a headline in our newspapers read: "Nuclear War Called Hazard to Public Health." When you consider that cigarettes and alcohol are hazardous to your health, you will be convinced that nuclear war is! In a recent letter of solicitation by a retired admiral for contributions to his laudable campaign for a nuclear freeze, I read: "During my seven-year stint in strategic planning in the Pentagon, I became acutely aware that nuclear weapons had created *a whole new ball game.*" The sportiveness of this remarkable insight is given scientific respectability in the next sentence: "They [the nuclear weapons] are a quantum jump," not to speak of the unintentional pun: a "ballgame" for a ballistics exchange is rather on the mawkish side. No *ad hominem* mockery is intended. The jaunty metaphor is one of myriad examples of our linguistic dilemma in the face of the world's nuclear madness.

A moralist might wish to adduce Socrates' admonition to Crito in Plato's *Phaedo*: ". . . you must know that to use words wrongly is not only a fault in itself, it also corrupts the soul." But, nowadays, even Socrates would scratch his head and concede: "there *are* no words accurate enough to describe what men have wrought." Words like "disaster" and "catastrophe" are too frivolous to describe a thermonuclear war, and the term "unacceptable damage" is a monstrous howler. It suggests that there *is* an acceptable damage, for instance if you drop a neutron bomb that silences people forever but leaves their telephone lines intact. Incidentally, the official term for a neutron bomb is "Enhanced Radiation-Reduced Blast" warhead. "To enhance" has a train of echos in it that suggests something salubrious like health or beauty; when linked with "radiation" it sounds grotesquely lugubrious.

Our sensibilities may further be nettled by the term "levels of redundancy" to denote our ability to kill each other several times over. If we consider that a nuclear bomb makes a rather big bang, not just a whimper, the bureaucratic cliché turns into a percussive metaphor. The "medieval" mind was preoccupied, as the saying goes, with the terpsichorean problems of how many angels could dance on the head of a pin, our "enlightened" mind with the problem of how many warheads we can crowd on a missile. We now have nuclear theologians!

To the linguistically sensitized folk, the many bloopers in our everyday speech produce a strange sensation—making one suddenly doubt one's familiar relationship with the language—not unlike the sense of disorientation aroused by the grotesque. Early in our century, the German poet Christian Morgenstern had adumbrated the vagaries of language in his nonsense verse, as had Brueghel in the sixteenth century in his illustrations of the linguistic quirks in proverbs. But in Morgenstern we can clearly discern an underlying moralistic intent: to be imprisoned in the clichés of language can be a most consequential, even dangerous, thing.

Even more insidious than our witless bloopers are the conscious lexical deceits perpetrated by military nomenclaturists. They have plundered classical mythology (*Jupiter, Apollo, Atlas, Orion, Ajax, Hercules, Zeus*), exploited the names of American heroes (*Davy Crockett, Minuteman, Pershing*), appealed to macho imagery (*Crusader, Mauler, Phantom, Redeye*) to "disarm"—linguistically!—the murderous threat posed by our war engines. These verbal efflorescences make earlier terms, such as "Flying-" or "Superfortress" sound naive and innocuous for being so direct. The linguistic trickery is at its most accomplished in pawning off the MX missile as a "Peacemaker."

These verbal palliatives stand in grotesque contrast to what they refer to and contain, undeniably, an element of political coercion. What Ezra Pound had to say about the function of literature and the responsibility of its practitioners in combating the corruptive moral influence of a corrupted language on politics and society may well serve as an admonition to our military lexicographers:

> Has literature a function . . . in the republic . . . ? It has. And this function is *not* the coercing or emotionally persuading, or bullying or suppressing people into the acceptance of any one set or any six sets of opinions . . .
>
> It has to do with the clarity and vigour of 'any and every' thought and opinion. It has to do with maintaining the very cleanliness of the tools, the health of the very matter of thought itself . . . the individual cannot think and communicate his thought, the governor and legislator cannot act effectively or frame his laws, without words, and the solidity and validity of these words is in the care of the damned and despised litterati. When their work goes rotten . . . the application of word to thing goes rotten, i.e., becomes slushy and inexact, or excessive or bloated, the whole machinery of social and of individual thought and order goes to pot. This is a lesson of history, and a lesson not yet half learned.[16]

We may have become inured to our inarticulate verbiage—the unintentional grotesqueries of our media-blabber, the linguistic gerrymandering committed by military strategists—but if in our more reflective moments we stop to think, we will certainly become aware of the grotesque cleavage between "signifier" and "signified," to use semiological babble. An increased sensitivity to our linguistic quandary may indeed help alert us to the pitfalls in our reasoning processes, for behind the inane or willful distortions of language looms a much greater crisis: the swamping of reason by the enormity of unreason.

In times of great chaos, we can observe the all too human tendency to reason oneself out of stubborn complexities into the redemptive promise of a simplicistic dogma, a cultist *idée fixe*, religious fundamentalism, a historistic or economic doctrine, what have you, all at the expense of informed personal judgment and responsibility, the two pillars of freedom. Dürrenmatt's drama, for instance, presents a whole rogues' gallery of monomaniacal would-be saviors who endow their principles of action with the rigidity of an alleged "absolute" truth, thereby only increasing the existing havoc. Their intent turns out to be a grotesque daemonic obsession born of the ludicrous illusion that they can see the world and human history from a transcendent vantage point. They themselves, if not the atrocities they commit, purportedly for the sake of a better world, may be susceptible to comic disarming, witness Charlie

Chaplin's *The Dictator* or Mel Brooks's Hitler in that waggish revue called "Springtime for Hitler" within his classic funny film *The Producers,* where he portrays the dictator as a flaccid acid-head with a languid "Jazz-Bo" drawl. However, Brooks's zany buffoonery lacks the sharp edge of the grotesque.

But perhaps more grotesque than the illusions of our simplicists are the convoluted rationalistic arguments of our martial theologians. We must accept an aggressive arms build-up for the sake of nonaggression, they say, which leads to the production of more and bigger and "better" bombs, with the avowed intent to make sure that they will never be used and we can live in peace of mind amidst ever more staggering "levels of redundancy." The spinning rationality of the supporting logistical arguments severely taxes the circuitry of a reasonable brain.

Joseph Heller again caught the essence of this mode of thinking or nonthinking in his *Catch-22,* the central idea of which has in itself become an overly used and, alas, trivialized catch phrase. The circuitous "reasoning" that Heller excoriates could be summarized as follows: to recognize a danger is the process of a rational mind. But the constant awareness of danger may drive one "crazy" to a point where one tries to eschew the threat. The ensuing anxiety, however, is an inverted proof for a sane mind. Ergo, we can and must embrace the danger—in insane sanity. The dizzying merry-go-round comes to a jolting halt in a monstrous inversion of the Categorical Imperative: "We must be prepared to do what we *ought not* to do." In a more appropriate metaphor: from its depth in the individual psyche the deadly vortex of Thanatos has spewed up an explosive paradox into our collective thinking. "Paradox" is an intellectual manifestation of the "grotesque" in the contemporary world; Dürrenmatt divined it more than two decades ago:

> . . . the grotesque is only a way of expressing in a tangible manner . . . the paradoxical, . . . and just as in our thinking today we seem to be unable to do without the concept of the paradox, so also in art, and in our world which at times seems still to exist only . . . out of fear of the bomb.[17]

One wonders what the great satirists of our common past—Pope, Swift, Voltaire, Mencken—would say to the skewed rationality rampant in our world.

Significantly, potent and sustained satire is rare or practically nonexistent in contemporary literature. Recently, the reviewer of some novels lamented that "the inability of satire and parody to lay hands on the public events of our time is an old, sad story" and then asks ingenuously: "What grotesque exaggeration could possibly add sardonic emphasis to the already distorted contours of everyday public life?"[18] While bemoaning the drying-up of the satiric vein in contemporary literature, he points in the right direction for its cause. Satire chastises, the grotesque exposes. Therefore, genuine satire can only thrive when we feel sure of the standards of reason to which we can refer. The best satire, namely that which is surest in tone, is precisely that which is also surest in its values, witness Pope who wrote in the Augustan Age of English literature, an epithet which in itself is a mark of confidence in the ideals of reason advanced by his age. If we excoriate unreason and obtuseness under the camouflage of irony or through the flank attack of innuendo, so common in satire, we must be sure of our reason, otherwise we court the dangers of mere self-righteousness (so obvious in the vituperations of some fundamentalists who know all the answers but none of the questions).

In our day, however, reason has been invaded by "rationales," "scenarios," "logistics," "game plans" fed into computers, culminating in the fatuous hope entertained by some naive enthusiasts that electronic intelligence will soon replace carbon intelligence even in the field of decision-making and value judgment, but also unleashing the fear in the rest of us that the new nonbiological "reason" might play some nasty tricks on us by giving the wrong signals to its counterpart on the other side. A grotesque inversion in our conceptual mode of thinking seems to be creeping in: human beings seen by the determinists of our time as the unwitting products of the brain's circuitry and of their "selfish genes"; computers as decision-making, autonomous intelligences. No wonder, Kurt Vonnegut suggests, that man is a "machine made out of meat."[19]

No doubt, reason is a many-splendored thing. The very term conjures up a good deal of semantic confusion, which in turn may lead, as it often has, to moral confusion. Those old-fashioned souls among us who still teach "humanities," against all odds and in endemic genteel poverty, feel that our world suffers increasingly from a dangerous cleavage between reason and mere reasonings, or call it "rationality." The dichotomy points to the difference between "doing" and "knowing," i.e., principles for reasonable, moral action on the one hand and the mechanism of understanding on the other, or normative and cognitive thought—hoary philosophic insights all too often ignored by those in power or drowned in petty academic disputes. The German philosopher Immanual Kant, perhaps more than any other, stressed the ability of "practical reason," as he called it, to make autonomous moral judgments on the basis of a priori insights, as opposed to the mere mechanistic absorption of sense data by our understanding. He had the advantage of being able to operate with the two German terms *Vernunft* and *Verstand*, a semantic distinction not so graphic in other languages, though it has not necessarily rendered speakers of German more *vernünftig*, than others. Kant also confidently postulated that the common man has spontaneous insight into the principles of morality without wading through a morass of philosophical argumentation exasperatingly sticky in his own works.

Fichte, an erstwhile disciple of Kant, in his philosophy of history, dramatically calls our age "The State of Completed Sinfulness,"[20] because it is lead astray by a misconceived rationality; and then he prophesies the inevitable dawn of a new age, when the "Science of Moral Reason" takes over. Maybe Kant's and Fichte's optimism about the spontaneity and efficacy of moral reason is justified. At least we can take some heart in the recent worldwide groundswell against nuclear madness and the Pope's strong moral indictment of continued weapons research.

I have tried to give an *aperçu* of some highlights in the theory and history of the modern grotesque, from its beginning in aesthetic play over its possible ontological and psychological implications to its contemporary sociological import and its manifestations in our language and the rational sphere. As we look back at my opening reference to the decorative grotesques, we may wonder: "How could that father give birth to this child?" Well, there is still a slight family resemblance. In its artistic and literary accouterment the grotesque still makes a strong appeal to the visual; then there is the outright assault on our anxiously guarded fields of familiarity—including perhaps a lingering moral sense—with its attendant alienating effect; but the primal pointlessness of the artist's aesthetic play with *form* has given way to the moralist's concern with the lack of ethical *norm*. And, finally, the lurking threat of Thanatos, the death instinct, has moved from its dark niche in the psyche into the deceptive light of our reasoning processes.

As we read Günter Grass and so many other writers of the grotesque mode, we might at first think that the point of view is too undefined, meanings so equivocal that they fade away like Cheshire cats. The equivocation is of course in keeping with the equivocal response of apprehension and laughter traditionally associated with the grotesque. But, in closing, we must ask ourselves what the purpose of the seemingly deadpan portrayal of dehumanizing atrocities in Malaparte, Heller, Dürrenmatt, and so many others is. It is no longer a mere comic disarming of an incipient threat so we can adopt a *noli me tangere* attitude and immediately relapse into our intellectual or emotional comfort. The workshop of grotesque writers is no dispensary for cheerful bromides. We might be tempted to say that their true intent is to illustrate the horrifying insight that the horrid can also be comical. But that seems too gratuitous and might apply at best to the manic humor of the likes of Monty Python, which is a way of coping with horror too enormous to confront openly, a protective maneuver similar to smoking a pipe, which gives one an aura of wisdom, while saying nothing. In that vein, the noncommittal stance of the literary grotesque in our day might be likened to the time-tested strategy of comedy, where the defense is complete and detachment from a potentially serious subject matter is achieved. But I doubt that.

In my view, the contemporary grotesque rather goes the opposite way: its aim is to arouse anxiety by means of the apparent comic and push it to a paroxysm, rather than allay our justifiable fears. In so doing, it need not indulge in flights of morbid fancy, but can gather up as in a focus the grotesque inherent in the world, in emblematic episodes that may function much as mathematical models do in describing empirical reality. In its contemporary garb the grotesque is a shock treatment to alert us to the moral chaos of our world. It provides no answers—didactic preachments would largely fall on deaf ears anyway—but it challenges us to find answers in thought and action by ourselves. Its apparent nihilistic cynicism is only the obverse of a positive moral revolt. If it expresses the guilty conscience of our age, in its clairvoyance it may also be the flipside of the prophetic, for to see the world as grotesque is not to see it as absurd, as incapable of change. The grotesque, far from identical with the restrictive and unconditional necessity inherent in the modern concept of the absurd, may direct human consciousness and imagination toward new and better possibilities.

The rules of classical rhetoric would now require a rousing, even uplifting peroration. But I cannot offer a soothing ointment for our anguish. I am too skeptical to believe in the luxury or ready availability of a simple redemptive doctrine. At best I can express a faint hope: the aggressive negativity of a grotesque consciousness may prick our moral sensibility to a point where in a precarious balance our reason may hold at bay the hellhounds of unreason. I might even venture a step in the direction of aesthetic optimism: the ensuing eternal vigilance may yet create a moral ambiance which will allow us to write genuine satire again in an age of relative reasonableness.

ACKNOWLEDGMENTS

I owe a debt of gratitude to many colleagues and friends at various institutions of higher learning who have greatly helped me in sharing my ideas on the grotesque, through their writings and their papers read at the "Grotesque"—Seminar of the Modern Language Association held in the 1970s, foremost among them Frances Barasch (Baruch College, CUNY), Arthur Clayborough (University of Trondheim, Norway), Arnold Heidsieck (University of Southern California), Lee B. Jennings (University of Illinois, Chicago Circle), Philip Thomson (Monash University, Melbourne, Australia).

NOTES

[1] Cf. G. Santayana, *The Sense of Beauty* (London, 1896), "Analysis of Grotesque Art," pp. 256–58.

[2] Cf. G. W. F. Hegel, *The Philosophy of Fine Art,* trans. F. P. B. Osmaston (London, 1920).

[3] Quoted by W. Kayser, *The Grotesque in Art and Literature,* trans. Ulrich Weisstein (Bloomington, 1963), p. 76.

[4] This is a formulation made current among critics of the grotesque by Lee B. Jennings in his *The Ludicrous Demon. Aspects of the Grotesque in German Post-Romantic Prose* (Berkeley/Los Angeles, 1963).

[5] W. Van O'Connor, *The Grotesque: An American Genre and Other Essays* (Carbondale, 1962), p. 14.

[6] T. Leary, R. Metzner, and A. Alpert, *The Psychedelic Experience: A Manual Based on the Tibetan Book of the Dead* (New Hyde Park, N.Y., 1964).

[7] In recent newspaper releases one could read that Professor Albert E. Millar Jr., Chairman of the English Department at Newport College, V.A., is running into some legal troubles with the producers of the film *E.T.* for suggesting in a published booklet that there are thirty-three parallels between E.T.'s terrestrial visit and the life of Christ. I wrote my lecture before I heard of Professor Millar's tribulations but was struck by the similarity between his perceptions and mine.

[8] M. Steig, "The Grotesque and Aesthetic Response in Shakespeare, Dickens and Günter Grass," in *Comparative Literature Studies,* 6 (1969), p. 178.

[9] G. Grass, *The Tin Drum* (New York, 1961), trans. R. Manheim, p. 202.

[10] For instance, in *The World According to Garp,* the film based on the novel by John Irving, the viewpoint remains equivocal in many episodes, as in the portrayal of the group of women who have their tongues cut out in painful and inarticulate protest against the trauma of statutory rape.

[11] C. Malaparte, *The Skin* (Boston, 1952), pp. 299–300.

[12] J. Heller, *Catch-22* (New York, 1955–65), pp. 347–48.

[13] I owe this reference to *Mad* to my friend Lee B. Jennings, who has kindly given me permission to use it.

[14] I read about this episode for the first time in a book review published in the *London Times Literary Supplement* (*TLS*) approximately two years ago, but could no longer locate the exact issue.

[15] F. Dürrenmatt, "Problems of the Theatre," trans. Gerhard Nellhaus, in *Four Plays 1957–62* (London, 1964), p. 33.

[16] Ezra Pound, "How to Read," in *Literary Essays,* p. 21.

[17] F. Dürrenmatt, ibid., pp. 33–34.

[18] R. M. Roberts in a review of Richard Sennett's *The Frog Who Dared to Croak* in *The New York Review of Books,* August 1982.

[19] Cf. G. Harpham, "The Grotesque: First Principles" in *Journal of Aesthetics and Art Criticism,* 34, 1975–76, p. 464.

[20] Cf. J. G. Fichte, *Grundzüge des gegenwärtigen Zeitalters,* trans. as *The Characteristics of the Present Age* (1844).

THE RAIN FALLS AND WE TURN TO REMEMBRANCE OF SENSORY THOUGHT

MICHAEL McCLURE

1

SURE, WE'RE EVERYTHING EXPLODING!
THE BIG-BLACK-BALL-BANG BLEW UP AND
WE'RE AT THE OUTER EDGE CURLING,
twisting into shapes of
penguins, Shelleys, sea urchins,
furling galaxies! SURE! I KNOW ALL THAT!
I see we're universes
overlapping, freed of time and space,
inventing new ones
while each dreams countless others
and their shadows are the shapes
of things! I KNOW ALL THAT
(AND
STILL
IT IS METAPHYSICS!)
I hear myself say,
"LANGUAGE FREES ME—CAN
DO SO—CAN LIBERATE ME!"
Yet, I don't believe it!
I don't feel those things!
I've been trained to see them,
TRAINED TO SAY THEM!

I'M

AS BLIND

AS AN ELF OWL TRAPPED

IN BLACK GRANITE

AND I'M
hungry!

I've lost the sight that lives and lingers
on the tips of fingers.

2

OH!

OH!

OH!

OH!

OH!

OH OH!

OH! OH!

OH, as the rain falls out there,
I'm falling too in front
of that waving tree of pink
plum blossoms. I'm crashing
down into the dirt and maybe
I'll rise up in spring flowers.
But, better yet, I'm here
to hold your soft dry foot—

to smell your sweet smell—
the scent that scatters from
your arms—to see your face

over and over—to know
you each morning—to
forever love you

in whatever time this is—
to worship the wrinkles round
your eyes—to know you in pain
or happy or suddenly

bursting into speech
like a songbird

a chickadee

that flies into the room!

The rain is spring burgeoning not gloom.

3
WHEN I WAS YOUNG, ON A DAY LIKE THIS
ALL POURING RAIN,
I'd go out to the farthest point of land
where it slipped into the ocean
from the cliffs and moisture seeped
from little springs, and I'd
cut pussywillows (dripping
glistening drops) and bring
them back for you and I
to eye-feast on in our poverty.
We'd stand them in a mason jar
and set them on an old black
wooden desk that was
a Grace within our
lives. Then

the catkins dried
and yellow pollen spread,
leaves came out,
and white snakey roots began to grow
in the bottom of the jar.
We were troubled
that we created a live
thing without a land.

NOW

I

KNOW

THAT

IS

LIKE

MY POETRY.

PORTFOLIO D: THE GOLDEN AGE OF GREECE, ETC.

JOAN RETALLACK

1.
eating with fingers out of communal bowl
animal motion
velocity of poetry
foreign affairs

got the
got the
got the
Chevy Chase Circle blues

this story old as time
devolution
fulguration
Dear———:

blanch and die
that is
Renaissance in England
regain balance before
Oresteia
Oresteia
family reunion

regain balance before
small instance
as it were

barking crow
pigpens and rumors of emeralds
not a
not a
not a
delicatessen
not an
intuition

Oshitashi
Oshitashi
not a game

despite
HA HA HA
canned laughter
HA HA HA
Academic Overture
HA HA HA
polyphonic powers

ostensibly of or set in countryside
yes
yes
yes
shepherds and other rural types
trees and streams
cows and sheep

all the while
monitoring inner distraction
idly turning pages
to
eliminate time
eliminate space

eliminate all 12 categories
facsimile first edition
O
illuminated manu-script
illuminated manu-script
these are the
graceful hoops
these are the
broad attempts
these are the
(slew Meaningless-Ness Monster)
these are the
Real Life
these are the
nervous giggle
these are the
monumental abandon
etc.

this is it
alright
this is it
sun is rising
this is it
Real Life
this is it
sun is setting
this is it
turn pages slowly
this is it
across great divide
this is it
passion
attachment
commitment
direction

HA HA HA
easily portable smile

HA HA HA
power on
HA HA HA
volume up
HA HA HA
pizza
HA HA HA
pizza with everything

power is on
volume is up
sun rises
sun sets
etc.

that is
just missed
that is
inside the
that is
she surely
that is
what?
that is
that he
that is
not his best
that is
perhaps
that is
meanwhile
that is
no doubt
that is
in some cultures
that is
screening applicants
that is
naming and knowing

that is
common knowledge
that is
Academic Overture
that is
1. the Spartan Lawgiver
2. Ethelred the Unready
3. the former capital of Russia
4. mouse-like rodents living in Mexico
5. buttered noodles peas and tofu
6. mountainous regions full of historical documents

2.
once said
better yet
left
EAT
double vision
this story old as time
what
one
is
not
circles
over
head
make faces
make fun of
make good
make out
make up

rest to Caprice
know what I mean?
fluted cups
bated breath
in short
quo animo?

tramping the Selkirk Mountains in B.C. we
nobody knew
invincible mispersuasion
rest to Folly
Folly and Caprice
paradigmatic grue-bleen phenomenon,
rest to Folly
Folly and Caprice

in the
blueberry barrens of Maine
she said
at the blowpipe

in the

blueberry barrens of Maine

she said

at the blowpipe

3.
bright window pane
'59 know what I mean
Greek food earthenware plates
logical construction of world
dotted line
bottom line
twixt Life and Death lies
dotted line
bottom line

smarting still

all parts can hear
the words

my fingers
can hear
the words
she says
my legs
my shoulders
my neck
my head

4.
blood starved facc of paradox
mountainous regions full of—
mouse-like rodents living in—
no indication of what is to follow

5.
this is it
monumental abandon
sun is rising
real life
sun is setting

small instance
as it were
barking crow
polyphonic powers
sun is rising

this is it
not a delicatessen
devolution
fulguration
regain balance before
sun is setting

graceful hoops
broad attempts

facsimile first edition
nervous giggle
sun is rising

eating with fingers
communal bowl
animal motion
sickening velocity
canned laughter
grave import
sun is setting
close of
business day

6.
sun rises
small instance
sun sets
as it
were
sun rises
polyphonic
powers
lose
feel
though
face
stung
glisten-
ing
sea
sun sets
one is *blind*
sun rises
effort
regain
sun sets
sun rises

quo animo?
take
eat
buttered noodles
sun sets
great
divide
sun rises
ah but
in short
sun sets
smile
slides
sun rises
make
out
faces
sun sets

THE AMUSEMENT PARK

JOSÉ EMILIO PACHECO

Translated from the Spanish by Katherine Silver

Labyrinthe, la vie, labyrinthe, la mort
Labyrinthe sans fin, dit le Maitre de Ho.
—Henri Michaux

1

The crowd has gathered around where the elephants are kept. Mercilessly, the men fight and insult each other: they are all trying to get to the front so as not to miss the slightest detail. Some of them, the younger ones, have climbed the trees and they watch the birth spectacle from there. The elephant is about to have a baby. She is infuriated by the pain and, bellowing, hits herself against the cement walls, throws herself on the ground, then gets up again. The male elephant and the people are mere spectators of the process. In her rage, the elephant does not allow the veterinarian or the trainer to approach her. Both, from a distance, anxiously await the outcome. Two hours pass. Finally—when the group of curious onlookers has grown into a multitude—a new body begins to emerge from within the old, dark body. The crowd, rejoicing in the elephant's pain, admires the birth of a monstrous beast, covered with blood and hair, that resembles an elephant. The animal staggers and appears to be about to fall. Suddenly it splits in two, the oilcloth cover deflates and from within springs a man dressed as a juggler who jumps around and does acrobatics while he rings two strings of jingle bells. The audience gives him a standing ovation and tosses coins that the man eagerly pockets. There is a new round of applause. The man thanks them with deep reverence. The two elephants curl up their trunks and lift up a leg. Some of the people in the audience want to whistle—but they are silenced.

2

The botanical garden is located at the other end of the park. Past the hot houses, beyond the cactus desert and the ninth lake and around a bend, a fictitious abundant growth appears. This place is dangerous and various policemen have been assigned by the park's management to keep guard. The clock strikes ten o'clock in the morning and a grammar school teacher, followed by a group of children, enters into the pretend jungle. The small woman greets the policemen by name and then, with a voice which attempts to be militaristic, orders the children to line up to the right. She asks the students Zamora and Lainez to come to the front. The teacher makes reference to their bad behavior, their lack of interest in their studies, the orange peal Zamora flung at her with a sling shot and the obscene gestures Lainez made when she turned her back to point out the mistakes he had made in an arithmetic problem he hadn't been able to solve on the blackboard. Without delay, the teacher grabs the students by their ears and, ignoring their pleadings and egged on by the applause and approval of the others and the guards' indolent attitude, pulls them over to the tentacles of the carnivorous plant. The plant swallows them up and avidly begins to suck them down. The only visible sign is the swelling in the stalk and the fierce peristaltic movements: one can imagine the suffocation, the work of the acid, the voracious dissolution of the bones. The teacher—resigned and bored—gives today's botany lesson *in vivo* and explains to her students that the carnivorous plant functions much like the digestive system of the boa constrictor. One boy raises his hand and while he looks distractedly at the plant which is now totally still, asks the teacher what a boa constrictor is.

3
I love Sundays in the park there are so many little animals I think I am dreaming or going crazy from so much pleasure and the happiness of always seeing so many different and fierce ones that play or make love or are always about to kill each other and it amuses me to watch them eat too bad they all smell so bad or in other words they stink no matter what they do to keep the park clean especially on Sundays the animals stink like hell nevertheless I think that they are just as amused seeing us as we are seeing them that is why I feel so much pity that they are always here their lives must be really hard always doing the same things so that the others will laugh or hurt them and I don't know how some of them can come in front of my cage and say look at the tiger doesn't he scare you because even if there were no bars I wouldn't make a move to attack them because, as everyone knows, I have too much pity for them.

4
The section euphemistically called the park's "kitchen" or "the workshops" are off limits to the spectators. Sights such as these could suddenly raise consciousness and even occasion subversive action. In a large patio enclosed by walls decayed by humidity, horses purchased at ridiculous prices are sacrificed to feed the beasts. The director, a humanitarian man, has prohibited the butchers' common brutal methods. But in sptie of this and since the subsidy the park receives barely covers the director's salary, benefits and travel money, the electric pistol has not yet been purchased and the slaughter is carried out by traditional methods: clubbings and beheadings. Old ones, under twenty years old, are continuously being liquidated on the patio. All meet their end here without consideration for their loyalty, their hours of service, their work capacity. Riding horses and work horses, old race horses, ponies and Percherons, are all united in death. When they can no longer be used, their owners sell them to the bull ring. If they do not meet with a horrendous death there, which, given the antecedents and the possibilities for the future, is finally an act of mercy, the horses are given the butcher's knife in payment for their efforts and infernal lives. Only bones, nerves and hides will be handed over to the carnivors' cages: in order to obtain additional

funds for the director, the least repulsive parts are sold to the hamburger and hot dog stands in the park, or are used to feed the indigent class of cats and dogs who dwell on the English lawns and Persian pillows. None of the park's workers or visitors mention the subject of the horses, perhaps because of an unconscious fear of unifying, establishing the connection, realizing that it is a metaphor, just barely exaggerated, for their own destinies.

5

Behind the cages stands the railroad station. A lot of children board the train, sometimes accompanied by their parents. They board enthusiastically and when the train pulls out they are taken aback and then joyfully watch the weeds, the forests, the artificial lake. The peculiarity of this train is that it never returns—and when it does, the children on board are already grown-ups who, as such, are filled with fear and resentment.

6

A family—father, mother and two boys—arrive in the park's grove and spread their blankets over the grass. The long awaited day in the country finally takes place this Sunday. One of the boys asks permission to go buy a balloon, and he walks away, crushing the broken leaves strewning the path. The man tells the woman to get lunch ready before the boy returns. The woman takes bread, butter, meat, and mustard out of the basket. Immediately, a few dogs gather around them and as usual, columns of ants advance towards the crumbs. The two adults love animals and have taught the child to feel the same way. So they begin to pass out crusts of bread and scraps of meat to the dogs and do nothing to prevent the ants from going into the basket where the flan and candies are kept. Within a short while, they are surrounded by seventy dogs and more or less a billion ants. The dogs demand more food. They howl and bare their fangs and the two adults and the child must throw their own morsels of food into the fauces. In the meantime, they are being covered by ants that voraciously, rapidly, giddily begin to tear them to pieces. When they become aware of their disadvantage, the dogs prefer to work together with the ants before it is too late. When the other child returns to the grove, he looks for his family and only finds the booty scattered about: long columns of ants (each insect carries an invisible piece of meat) and an orgy of dogs play at burying tibias and skulls and make an effort to tear apart the tiny skeleton that finally gives way and just one instant later, falls apart.

7

In the shade of the mechanical games, stands the monkeys' island. A moat and a fence separate them from those who, with irony and pity, watch them live. In the wilds of the jungle, known only to the first generation (now extinct) of park inmates, the monkeys lived in peace and scarcity, without oppressing the inferior members of their species. In their over-populated captivity, they take advantage of whatever they can. The tension, the aggressive cohabitation, the lethal noise, the lack of pure air and space, forces them to consume tons of bananas and peanuts. A few times a day, terrified and armed men must clean out the island completely so the garbage and shit does not suffocate its inhabitants. In this way, the monkeys have their survival guaranteed: they need not look for food, and the veterinarians (when they can) cure their wounds and diseases. Nevertheless, existence on the island is sinister and brief. The prison system is based on a merciless hierarchy that allows the leaders of the community to become tyrants. Good gamesters but cowards by nature, the chimpanzees' only duty is to act like buffoons to entertain those inside and outside. The ethnic minorities, such as the howler monkey, the titi monkey and the spider monkey, live in atrocious servitude. The mandrills spend their time worshipping the gorillas and nobody bothers to care for the young: prostitution and perversion corrupt all at a tender age, and the number of crimes increases daily. Incapable of rebelling against man who, by capturing them, destroyed their wild paradise and brought them, numbed and half-dead, in iron chains to the park, the monkeys destroy each other and many end up deceiving themselves by believing that the horrors of the island are the natural order of the world, that things always were and will continue to be this way, and that the circle of stones and the fence are insurmountable. Perhaps one little outbreak of insurrection would be enough to make everything different.

8

The architect who planned this park had read the novel about the man who was put on exhibit in a zoo, and decided to do something much more original. His idea has been so successful that they have tried to copy it everywhere (without success) and *Life* magazine in Spanish dedicated eight color pages to it. Following are the architect's statements published in *Life* magazine: "The amusement park I have given to my city is certainly not original but it is perhaps surprising. The park appears to be like any other: it is visited by people anxious to contemplate the three kingdoms of nature: but this park contains another park, which (by inverting the process of certain bottles which can be emptied but not filled again), can be entered even when all possibility of exit is closed off (unless of course the visitors attempt to dismantle an entire system which the theory of some Chinese boxes applies to monumental architecture), since this second park is contained within another park in which the visitors contemplate those who contemplate. And the third, in turn, is within another park where the visitors contemplate those who are contemplating those who contemplate. And that is within another park, contained in another park in another park within another park—just the first links in an infinite chain of parks that contain more parks and are contained within parks within parks when nobody sees anybody without at the same time being watched, judged and condemned. To illustrate what I mean, let's take a simple and immediate example. Look: the crowd has gathered around where the elephants are kept. Mercilessly, the men fight and insult each other: they are all trying to get to the front so as not to miss the slightest detail. Some of them, the younger ones, have climbed the trees, and they watch the birth spectacle from there. The elephant is about to have a baby. She is infuriated by the pain and, bellowing, hits herself against the cement walls, throws herself on the ground, then gets up again. . . .

IDEOGRAMS IN CHINA

HENRI MICHAUX

Translated from the French by Gustaf Sobin

To Kim Chi

Lines going off in all directions. In every which way: commas, loops, curlicues, stress marks, seemingly at every point, at all levels: a bewildering thicket of accents.

Cracks, claw marks: the very beginnings appear to have been suddenly checked: arrested.

Without form, figure, or body, without contour, symmetry, or center, without evoking any known property whatsoever.

Without any apparent rule of simplification, unification, generalization.

Neither stripped nor refined, lacking sobriety.

Each seems, at first sight, as if scattered.*

Ideograms devoid of all evocation.

* What, as apparent scribble, was once compared to the tracks of insects or the erratic footprints of birds upon sand still conveys, unchanged, perfectly legible, comprehensible, and efficacious, the Chinese language, the oldest living language in the world.

Characters of an unending variety.
The page, containing them, like a lacerated void.
Lacerated by a multitude of undefined lives.

There was a time, however, when the signs still spoke, or nearly; when, already allusive, they revealed—rather than simple things or bodies or materials—groups, ensembles, situations.

There was a time . . . There were others, as well. Without making any attempt to simplify or condense, each period obfuscating for its own particular sake, setting things to rout, learned how to manipulate the characters, to separate them even further—in some new way—from their original reading.

Interval.

What won out, finally, was the tendency to conceal. Reserve, prudence won out, a natural restraint, and that instinctive Chinese habit of covering one's tracks, of avoiding exposure.

What won out was the pleasure of remaining concealed. Thus the text, henceforth, covert, secret: a secret between initiates.

A long and involved secret, not readily shared, the requisite for belonging to that society within a society. That circle which, for centuries, would remain in power. That oligarchy of the subtle.

The pleasure of abstraction won out.
The brush freed the way, and paper made the going easier.

One could now readily abstract from the original reality, from the concrete and its closely related signs; could abstract, move swiftly with abrupt brushstrokes that slid, unhesitating, across the paper, giving Chinese an entirely new appearance.

Withdrawal, self-absorption won out.
Won out: the will to be mandarin.*

Gone, now, were those archaic characters that had stirred the heart. And those signs, so palpable, that had overwhelmed their own creators and amazed their very first readers.

Gone, too, were the veneration and simplicity, the earliest poetry, the tenderness that arose from the surprise of the first "encounter." Gone, the still "pious" brushstroke and the gliding ease. (Still absent, yet to come, the intellectuals with their deft tracings: the tracings of intellectuals . . . of scribes).

All contact cut, now, with the beginnings . . .

Innovating, at first, with prudence, but with a growing disrespect and with the joy at seeing that "it worked," that one was still being followed, understood . . .

Carried away by the seductive effrontery of their own pursuits, the inventors—those of the second period—learned how to detach the sign from its model, deforming it cautiously, at first, not yet daring to sever form from being: the umbilical, that is, of resemblance. And, in so doing, detached themselves, rejected the sacred from that earliest equation: "word-object."

* Diminished, deformed as they are, these characters, illegible to hundreds of millions of Chinese, never entirely lost their meaning. Excluded from the inner circle of the literate, the peasantry looked upon these characters without, admittedly, understanding them, but sensing nonetheless that they came from the same place as themselves: those nimble signs, predecessors to the incurvated rooftops, to dragons and theatrical figures, to cloud drawings and landscapes with flowering branches and bamboo leaves, all of which they'd seen in pictures and knew how to appreciate.

Religion in writing was on the decline; the irreligion of writing had just begun.

Gone, now, were the "heartfelt" characters, so dependent upon reality. Vanished from usage, from language. They remained, however, upon the slabs of the oldest tombs, on the bronze vases dating from the earliest dynasties. Remained, too, upon divinatory bones.

Later, those early characters, sought after everywhere throughout the Middle Kingdom, meticulously compiled and recopied, were interpreted by scholars. An inventory, a dictionary of original signs, was established.

Rediscovered,
and rediscovering, at the same time, the emotion inherent in those calm, tender, tranquil first writings.

The characters, restored to their original meanings, came back to life.

In this perspective, any written page, any surface covered with characters turns into something crammed and seething . . . full of lives and objects, of everything to be found in the world, in the world of China,

full of moons and hearts, full of doors
full of men who bow
who withdraw, grow angry, and make amends
full of obstacles
full of right hands, of left hands
of hands that clasp, that respond, that join forever
full of hands facing hands
of hands on guard, and others at work
full of mornings
full of doors
full of water falling, drop by drop, out of clouds
of ferryboats crossing from one side to another

full of earth embankments
of furnaces
of bows and runaways
and full, too, of disasters
and full of thieves carrying stolen goods off under their arms
and full of greed
and meshed armor
and full, too, of true words
and gatherings
full of children born with a caul
and holes in the earth
and of navels in the body
and full of skulls
and full of ditches
and full of migratory birds
and newborn children—and so many!
and full of metals in the depths of the earth
and full of virgin land
and fumes rising from swamps and meadows
and full of dragons
full of demons wandering across the open country
and full of everything that exists in the world
such as it is or assembled in some other fashion
chosen deliberately by the inventor of signs that they be
brought together
scenes that lend themselves to reflection
scenes of all sorts
scenes that proffer a meaning, or several meanings,
that they be submitted to the spirit
that they issue forth:
clustered that they might end in ideas
or unravel as poetry.

Part of that original treasure remains lost. There still exist, however, enough etymologies of an indisputable nature to permit an accomplished scholar to recognize often, running throughout, the particular origins and—in the instant of tracing the characters in their present form—to draw inspiration from the distant past.

No matter how far removed the new character is from the old, the scholar can still bring fresh life to the object by means of the word.

This is the direction he's drawn in, what his graphics aim for.

He needs no further skills—thanks to the nuance of his subtle brushstrokes.

Chinese: a language perfectly suited for calligraphy.* One that induces, provokes the inspired brushwork.

The sign, without insistence, allows one to return to the object, to the being that, in the running text, need only be inserted into this expression quite literally expressive.

For ages the Chinese had been subject, in this field and others, to the charm of resemblance: to an immediate resemblance, at first, and then to a distant one, and finally to the composition of resembling elements.

An obstacle, as well: it had to be overcome.

Even that of the furthest resemblance. There was no returning; all similitude was to be abandoned forever.

Another destiny awaited the Chinese.

To abstract means to free oneself, to come disentangled.

* Rather than calligraphy, the art of writing. With the exception of Arabic, calligraphy in other languages (when it exists) is no more than the expression of either some psychological order or, during great periods, of some ideal and often religious comportment. There is in all that a rigidity, a stiffness, a uniform stiffness that produces lines, not words, the standard corset of nobility, liturgy, of puritanical severity.

The destiny that awaited Chinese writing was utter weightlessness.

The characters that evolved were better suited than their archaic predecessors in terms of speed, agility, deftness of gesture. A certain kind of Chinese landscape painting demands speed, can only be executed with the same sudden release as the paw of a springing tiger. (For which one must first be concentrated, self-contained and, at the same time, relaxed).*

The calligrapher, likewise, must first be plunged in meditation, be charged with energy in order to release: to discharge that very energy. And all at once.**

The necessary knowledge—the "four treasures" of the writer's chamber (brush, paper, ink, and inkstone)—is extensive, complex. But then . . .

The hand should be empty, should in no way hinder what's flowing into it. Should be ready for the least sensation as well as the most violent. A bearer of influx, of effluvia.

. . . In a certain way similar to water, to both its lightest and most vigorous properties, its least apparent, such as ripples,*** which have always been a subject of study in China.

Even before the advent of Buddhism, water—the image itself of detachment, bound to nothing and ready, at every instant, to continue its course—spoke to the very heart of the Chinese people. Water, the absence of form.

* Meditation, the inner communion before a given landscape, might last twenty hours and the execution of the painting no more than twenty or thirty minutes. Here, then, is a painting that leaves room for space.

** The tiger's leap, even in religion. In Ch'an, in Zen, what stuns is the instantaneity of the illumination.

*** Deep ripples or shallow ones, ripples of water running or falling in waterfalls to re-emerge, bubbling, on the surface. Certain painters are famous for their water ripples, as the venerable Wang Wei for having discovered the ripple "of the rain and snow."

Yi Tin, Yi Yang, tche wei Tao
Alternately Yin, alternately Yang
This is the way; this, the tao.

The way traced by writing.

To be a calligrapher, as one might be a landscape painter. Even better, for in China a calligrapher is considered the salt of the earth.

In this particular calligraphy—this art of the temporal, expressing as it does trajectory, passage—its most admirable quality (even more than its harmony or vivacity) is its spontaneity. This spontaneity runs, sometimes, to the point of shattering.

No longer to imitate, but signify nature. By strokes, darts, dashes.

Ascesis of the immediate, of the lightning bolt.

The sign in Chinese, today, which is no longer in any way mimetic has the grace of its own impatience. It has drawn from nature its flight, its diversity, its inimitable way of knowing how to bend, rebound, redress itself.

Like nature, the Chinese language does not draw any conclusions of its own, but lets itself be read.

Its meager syntax leaves room for guesswork, for creativity, leaves space for poetry. Out of the multiple issues the idea.

Characters open onto several directions at once.

Point of pure equilibrium.

Every language is a parallel universe. And none more lovely than Chinese.

Calligraphy enhances it, for it completes the poem, is the expression that gives the poem its validity and, at the same time, vouches for the poet.

An exact balance between opposites, the art of the calligrapher (both in its separate steps and overall procedures) consists in revealing himself to the world. Like a Chinese actor entering on stage and giving his name and birthplace, then relating what has happened and what he is about to do, the calligrapher envelopes himself in his own motivations, furnishes his own justifications. It is apparent, in calligraphy, by the way one handles signs whether one is truly lettered, is truly worthy of the art. By this criterion alone, one is—or is not—justified.

Calligraphy in its role as mediator between communion and abeyance.

What might have happened if some Western language had had even a fraction of the calligraphic possibilities as Chinese? The baroque that would have ensued, along with the happenstance discoveries of individualists, all the rarities and peculiarities, the eccentricities of every possible kind.

Chinese was equal to all of this. Everywhere it offers up new possibilities; its every character serves as a fresh temptation.

If one takes, from various authors, a specific character, one that is easily recognizable, attractive, and charged with sense, and detaches it from both text and context, the word "heart" for example, no matter how far removed the brushstrokes might be from anything that might resemble a heart, the heart will, nonetheless, by its tracing, take on—with each calligrapher—a particular life of its own. One can readily see, among various calligraphers, how each time it is the same, and each time entirely different. One heart is generous, and another high-spirited. One heart would deceive while yet another would welcome: be good to live with. There is a heart at deep peace with itself, and a heart that is warm, well-disposed. Or the heart unruffled, that nothing troubles, that saves its own skin every time. Or one that is fickle, that settles nowhere, or another that is fearsome, and still another, submissive. There is a heart, too, that—at the drop of a hat—would take flight. Or the meddlesome heart, or the heart expectant, or venturous, or dry, or placid, or—to the contrary—the dauntless heart that nothing can stop. Or the entirely attentive, the perfect heart that even on a fibrous sheet of rice paper can last centuries and still manage to astonish.

To every calligrapher, the life, the proprietorship of the heart is offered. But not for the sake of originality, unless it be muted, unless he himself be scarcely suggested.

It is considered base, vulgar to behave ostentatiously.

Only the "exact placement," the "just proportion" matter.

And the perfect page is the one that "seems traced at a single go."

China, righteous and mindful as it was of harmony, would have scarcely appreciated the buffoon.

Writing must possess an invigorating quality. For writing is a way of life.

A perfect, an exemplary balance must be maintained. Even among those fanatics, commonly called "the madmen of calligraphy," who went without eating, drinking, and sleeping, and who had lost all sense of measure in their lives, the very instant they picked up their brushes, they would trace characters entirely free of any imbalance; characters, to the contrary, filled with a new and masterful equilibrium.
The highest order is always dynamic.

And so Chinese writing was saved from both the rigid and the baroque,* the two traps of calligraphy.

* Free calligraphy.
In Japan, all kinds of freedom have been taken and new pleasures derived from excessive practices in calligraphy. This freedom might, someday—who knows?—swarm across all of Chinese Asia.

China, land where one meditated upon the tracings of a calligrapher as, in other countries, one would meditate upon a mantra, or upon substance, essence, or fundamental principles.

Calligraphy around which—quite simply—one might abide as next to a tree, or a rock, or a source.

THE FOURTH OF JULY

ANDREI CODRESCU

I know a sad and large man who lives in West Germany.

That's how I thought I would start a newspaper article about a man I don't know, a Romanian poet who sends me his sad self-published little books every three months or so. This man is a doctor, a G.P. probably, in a small coal-mining German town. I see the post office where he buys his stamps and gets his mail and the little coffee shop where he has his *schwartze Kaffee* and writes his sad poems. His poems aren't just sad, they are desolate, they are haunted, they are hollow and ground down, the despair is thick and incontrovertible. There are leaden seas and hopeless rivers in them and burnt trees with dots of pain on the charred branches. The humans are missing from his landscapes as resolutely as if they'd been rubbed out so long ago nobody even remembers them. But once in a while, a remarkable little human thought will make its appearance, astonishing in its petty incomprehension. Things like: "They've thought of it so now I have to eat it." Does he have a wife, children? Probably.

Today is the Fourth of July. The radio plays the "To Anacreon in Heaven," from which F. S. Key took "The Star-spangled Banner." I'm an American, no doubt about it. My heart swells with pride at this brass riot, I am transported. I love Mr. Jefferson. A genius. A revolutionary. A great visionary. He would have puked on Ronald Reagan. He would have put little Ronnie on one of his enormous, historical knees and puked the remains of an immense vegetarian meal washed down with grog on Ronnie's little head. Ronnie should be so lucky!

Whenever I go into a school, I try to get maximum erotic charge from youth, so I compose odes which correct the obvious inconvenience of actual bodies and their deformities. Only rarely among youth, in schools, do you actually *see* a shining body or mind. You just suspect that they are there, because they *have* to be. So sayeth all of folklore. So sayeth your old mind. So you bring out these things that all these things sayeth by means of odes.

Always use their typewriters
They will never be the same
Stoned keys the silent arbiters
Of dangers hidden in a name.

Not that the poem comes out best
In jail, but under the piano or
In the dusty street where the rest
Roll back eggs into the nest

Of a fact in the sidebar of a news-
Letter being put together by young
Bodies complicated not obtuse
Transparent, sincere, oh skinny tang!

How silly. But you can bring out youth by these semihermetic means, if only because curiosity makes a creature bloom. But I'm not even being amused. I simply suffer the ignominy of cuteness, the futility of pretending something for a bit, a tiny bit of money. Meanwhile, the children, the bodies I am teaching, are immensely rich. Half the children are millionaires themselves, the other half's parents are. There are Mercedes, Cadillacs, Jaguars parked in the school lot. You can hear a kind of content gurgle, the flowing of milk through the well-worn channels of oligarchic tranquility. There are names here that go back to the founding days of the Republic, traditions tighter than a harness on a cavalry horse. The military, business, and managerial castes have money riding on these children. Indeed, they ride *on* money, like wagons on rails. The youth I am trying to bring out is the youth that is being ground out of them by means of a rigorous education. The forms of youth are set, the manifestations coded, the clothes ascribed, the limits defined. I'm a fool, in the English office, with an old typewriter.

I can imagine this little West German doctor, this terrible poet, this sad caricature in Germany, the Germany of the post-post-miracle. The burghers are only now awakening from the postwar miracle, and they find themselves to be little Americans! Cubed houses, disposable cars, fast food! But they are only formally Americans, Americans without Mr. Jefferson. Inside, they are nobody. At the center of the nobodiness of their hollow inside sits this sweating little immigrant, this sloppy fat doctor writing his desolate, horrid, hopelessness-filled works. He is like a wafting of bombed basement this little foreigner, his dark eyes darting between one hollow breast to another of the masectomized owner of the little café where he likes his *schwartze Kaffee* hot. He knows that her breasts are only rubber balloons, he had ordered them for her by mail, and he adjusts them every month.

The radio hostess was so-o-o thrilled to have me on her show. It was like having a doll or a a new dress, something so-o-o exciting! I had it in my mind to make her laugh. It was, ultimately, too easy. She was already laughing when I went in. She laughed all the way through the introduction, then laughed at her own question, then literally *cracked up*—her make-up opened up like an earthquake into myriads of gray lines—and she *kept* cracking up . . . it was epic, completely out of proportion with what I heard myself saying, which was nothing. "Read to me," she said, "something from your pockets." I'd just told her that my pockets were filled with art, notes, poems, that they were veritable mines full of treasures, all one had to do was dig, dig. I put my hands into the left mine, pushed past South Africans with headlights, and pulled this out, and read:

"All have secrets who have experienced inexpressible things. A secret is what has no language. Morons have the most secrets. The NSC and the CIA, which have the most secrets, are the world's biggest morons. After that, come poets, who are forever struggling with the inexpressible, and are only capable of small portions of it, meager meals to be sure."

"Oh! OH! That's so-o-o! Read it again, please!"

I read:

"Everything is inexpressible. Morons are walking bombs bursting with secrets. We sat down at a meal of filet moron and were quickly imbued with mystery, soaked in essence, perforated by the elsewhere."

Behind the twinkling eyes of the radio hostess, the automatic question-making machine broke down, and for a moment the wires showed. Through the cracks in her make-up I saw someone squatting on the ground in August, making peepee, while enormous black clouds covered the earth. Soon, it was going to rain.

Kansas is as big as the world.

Either I have been blessed with content or cursed with it. Whichever way you look at it, it's work. Without content it's easier work, dependent on other means of support, some of them truly undignified. With content it's a mixture of work and some of the easiness of noncontent. The payoff of content is fame, money, immortality, a seat at the circus.

Like flowers growing out of thin air, or enormous vegetables in outer space, with their roots showing like the obscene nerves of molars, the little West German exile's poems grow and scintillate with a life of their own, nourished by a deep fake memory, no talent and no music, in and of themselves like Leibnitz's spheres. He admires their growth, despises himself, bows to the other customers. It's closing time at the sad café in the sad little provincial town in little America Germany. Everyone now must go home to their cement cubes to turn on the TV. The proprietress thrusts her rubber balloons provocatively forward as she wipes the spot of dry *schwartze Kaffee* on the marble top. With a sudden gesture the poet sticks his fork into one of them. It deflates with a sad hiss, letting out sad years of marital juggling, pastel dreams, a variety of mouths stuck at various angles of greed, their teeth shining and showing, and air. "Oh, mein Gott!" mumbles the terrified poet. "Frau Goebbels! I didn't mean to!" He takes his poor head between his sweaty, trembling palms, and with a resolute gesture, pulls it off his neck, and in the same movement, lifts the blouse of the proprietress and sticks it in there where the deflated breast can be heard breathing its last pfffssst! It is, needless to say, a huge head, completely out of proportion with the other rubber breast, giving her, momentarily, a grotesque appearance. It has all happened so fast! Frau Goebbels is so astonished, she has not stopped wiping the spot of *schwartze Kaffee* on the marble top. But it's a fact: the head of the poet is now the left breast of the café owner. And there is terrible disproportion between left and right, a kind of monstruous political imbalance possible only in Germany.

I meet a friend of mine for coffee downtown. This friend of mine is a poet who has been in school for a very long time. He has a degree in poetry, he writes a very precise kind of poetry that is very much like the poetry other school poets write. His poetry is very comical, actually, but he thinks of it as at least profound, if not tragic. He is all worked up over a parable he has found in a story by Borges, a parable that concerns him personally.

It appears that a king had commissioned a poetic battle from a poet. The poet came back with a great poem full of great poetic victories. The king gave him a mirror, told him to go away. Ten years later, the poet returns with the battle. He reads it to the king, and it *is* the battle. The King gives him a gold mask. The poet goes away for another ten years, whispers something in the king's ear, and kills himself. The king gives up kinging, becomes a beggar, and wanders about in rags.

"And," my friend said, "I'm now working to become perfect at the battle, so I could get the mask!"

I felt suddenly very sorry for him. All that schooling—wasted. All that dedication—coming to naught.

"Listen," I said, "that mask is only a medal of service. The poet had only managed to return the mirror to the king so the king could see himself. So he gave him a medal of service to the state because he'd finally learned how to politick and flatter. Alas, the poet was only a poet when he brought in the first poem. After that, he was only a courtier and a vassal."

"How about the last part?" the poet protested vehemently, "Isn't the king wise to give up? And isn't the poet wise?"

"That last part is disgusting," I said. "Of course, old men become wise. What else can they become with a foot, a hand, and a tongue in the grave? Still, the poet is wiser than the king because he has the good sense to go in search of the unknown. The king just walks around hoping to hear from the dead, which is probably what the poet promised him, that he would come back in another ten years with the news, if not a new poem. And the fool king believes him."

"That's terrible," the poet says. "Do you want to talk about something else?"

Never. I never want to talk. I throw the waitress an evil look, and leave.

The proprietress, left hanging there with uneven breasts, faced the West German without a head, trying in vain to look into his eyes. She would have done better to lift her blouse and look into his eyes there. But then a miracle happened. The head began to shrink. No, the other breast began to grow. No, the head began to shrink. No. And so on. I could care less.

A sudden rain is going to drown out the fireworks at the harbor. But the radio goes on, playing my song.

FROM A GAZEBO

PAUL HOOVER

1

Matins for some and curtains for
others. No birds sing. But then,
of course, it's fall. Birds don't
sing in the cold. They just go away,
and the wind strikes bricks and alleys
like office noise that keeps the
workers nervous or the struggles of
a sheep I found caught in a fence
and which, like Frank Sinatra, suavely
limped away. Yes, metaphor leads us
astray, to little lambs lost in the
woods and blue-eyed maidens waiting,
La Belle Dame and Daisy. But never
mind all that. Morning is sunny
and calm. The El train rumbles by,
eye-level with the window, though at
a respectable distance, so it's less
threat than art. Sometimes at night
it passes with its little panels
of light containing upright figures
like people in toy airplanes who
raise their shrieking hands. And
come to think of it, what must we

look like, framed in our night windows?
It's simply morning now, and somewhere
in its whiteness there is a shadowless
truth Plato might have liked. A truck
pulls up with beer, and two stout
gentlemen cart in ten red boxes with
"Stroh's" written on the sides. Steam
issues from a pipe: the laundromat
is open, where all the tough kids hang:
a city neighborhood where no one owns
a gazebo, and the prettiest thing one
sees is concrete when it rains. Oh,
dry and boring day, with my fever for
conquest unquenched, how can I go on
thinking? Have I said what saying
gives me, or am I in my mind, so notably
feeble in spite of querulousness that
suggests a kind of strength? (1. Knowledge
of subject matter 2. Written and oral
communication 3. Qualities of leadership
4. Dependability 5. Ability to plan
and organize 6. Relationships with others.
All of the above may be evaluated in
the following categories: Above Average,
Average, Below Average, Not Observed.
You may add additional pages if the
space provided does not prove sufficient.
Please sign your name at the bottom,
neither bluntly nor ornately.) I was
thinking, the other day, about a woman
I dated who later joined the Army. She'd
drag me off to Mass (fat chance of my
conversion) at Holy Name Cathedral
where cardinal's hats are strung from the
ceiling. We like such quaint traditions
perhaps *because* they're passing, but
the hats don't seem to care whether
or not we care. They sway in the windy
cathedral. Caught in a bramble of

thought (that is, what was thought by
Scotus, Maritain) even a theologian
finds room for one more thought, bound
in its own tradition like a thousand
years of Latin. Matins, not midnight.
The gruesome matinee from which one
always emerges, surprised at the light
he finds. Morning stands for promise,
not sullen disappointment, so I lift
all spells of dread like scenery in
a play, and if I could sing with
heartbreaking tenor, I'd offer a song
to it. Aubade. The morning glory.

2

But that's not all. As our morning
song goes to pieces in a mist of
cigarettes, other flirtations occur,
though at a sparring distance. Koren
sobs at the window because her leaving
mother, with many things in mind, forgot
to turn and wave. Don't worry, kid,
she loves you. Hey someone, come
around. Drop in. Have a ball. Let's
cut the rug sometime. Hey, you wanna
beer? Turn on the lights, it's dark.
Put on your old pink dress with the
deep décolletage and your fluffy
high-heeled slippers: we'll dance
to brittle records and hit the hot motel
with its sizzling bar and grill and
size-ten dance floor packed. For breakfast
I had some coffee, pecan coffee cake
(one-sixteenth of it), and a glass of
orange juice made from concentrate.
The cake itself was sugar, pecan nuts,
nonfat milk and water, eggs, raisins,
filbert nuts, citron, lemon, orange,
salt, monoglycerides, yeast, dextrin,

artificial flavors, peanuts, walnuts,
calcium sulfate, sodium stearyl
lactylate, potassium sorbate, spice,
and coloring. Oh, yes, cottonseed oil.
It's terribly important. Say, isn't
this awfully droll? Who cares what's
in the cake? But I could feel your
interest as the list was being given.
Is he going to put "rat shit"? And you
derived some pleasure, however modest,
from the common details of life.
A lamp on during the day, especially
out of doors, is the kind of thing
I mean, or someone wearing mismatched
shoes, one high-heel and one ski boot.
But it needn't be that weird. A pebble
inside a Bible. Sun on a Panama hat.
My eyes rolling up in my head like
those statues on Rhodes which stood
looking out from niches. I'm made
from standing sand that's held up
by pure will, and even that is sifting.
Once I saw a movie in which a woman
held up a bottle of sand, exclaiming,
"It's from Los Alamos, the atom testing
site. It breeds by itself; every six
weeks or so, you got to dump some out.
It drifts inside the bottle." I was
thinking, too, of a man on television
who wears a beard of bees. He straps
the queen in a box just beneath his
chin, then workers and drones will
gather. The first bad thought and
he's dead, but he walks blithely around
and kisses his wife on the lips. She
has to put up with the guy. His whole
life's been these bees. They buzz
around his smile, nestle on the pillow.
The kids are used to Dad swarming in

his rocker: "What's on TV, kids?"
It's Mr. Moto or something: they mumble
what they say. Maybe the neighbors
grumble, but I say he's a hero—the man
is never nervous! Today I thought
it would snow, but it only rained, and
now at 3:21, while Koren is learning
to swim, bobbing ten feet deep, eyes
closed against the water, I end my little
dictation which grows like bottled sand.

3

The mind has sexes, too, and the
shifting from one to another is a
little like treading water with hands
held over your head. A parrot saying
"parrot." A blue chair on the veranda
(piazza, gallery) where Neruda rolls
with the girl on a seamless marble
slab, not in mystic pleasure but
gruntingly pounding each other through
blue serge, cotton, and lace. You, me,
us, them, we, our, nor, stare, collar,
holder, ivy, never, leisure, angle,
curfew, furlough, feather, eager—all
of it concerns, disabled, *deshabille*.
But let me reassure you, in spite of
a French word heard, I've had my picture
taken with a decomposing group back
where clotheslines freeze, and my
farmboy bowl haircut still shapes the
way I stand with lyrical intentions
created from mud and desire (and an
average sense of relations) into nets
of words. It's nice being me, I imagine.
I accept the role with genial desperation.
My Desi Arnaz hair, James Dean crease
in the pants, Hermione Gingold manner,
Don Ameche teeth, Broderick Crawford

neck, and Jack Paar piercing look—
all lend a certain "don't know what"
to this gavotte of pedants and cynical
lack of events, as if we'd suddenly sunk
into Louisa's dream, neither oblique
nor elliptic, but directly terrified
by swimming horses and knives creating
bland traditions. I was born in Virginia
to modest professional parents. Religion
was part of our life. Used to mow the
lawn. Used to practice golf. Once
I saw a fox. (And here the memory fails,
as if a staggering man carrying a panel
crossed Hollywood and Vine between the
light and sight.) Kept from stern
elations by sterner weaknesses, one
chooses to live in the present, with
its counter suppositions like Jarvis
Liquor Stores. No nonfiction? No.
As Clausewitz once said, "War is
very simple, but it is also very
difficult." The same may be said
of life, that we love its deprivations,
so impeccably idiotic, that make us glad
for a sandwich and maybe cookies later.
My life consists of a shy acceptance
of just about everything—that is,
a sense of the worthless as having
a grim importance I can never equal:
a ball of string, for instance, that
gathers over the years, or dust growing
in a corner in roughly the shape of
a cat. Still, the reader gladly admits
admiring himself in the text, holding it
like a mirror so later he might say,
"That was me as a youth, careless
and contented, with adventure on my
mind," for the self is a topic that
never grows stale and nourishes like

bread. Even shattered glass expresses
gleeful Me to some marquis's child.
Still, it might be rather pleasant
to sit in simple quiet, my silence
only broken by certified nods of the
head, as I grow inwardly solid like
monuments taking shape. The sun goes
over twice, shadows spread and fade,
and pallidness is suggested by the
reader's "monastic" position as unicorn
attendant in a sweet medieval farce
not unlike television. The smuggest
view of life is yet unpioneered, and
though we're drawing closer, centuries
await with arrogance unimagined, rocking
out of cradles. Whatever we get said
won't turn the planet faster. The
crowd grows amorous as events on the ledge
take place, the weather of the language.

4
Koren sleeps on the floor because
there's nothing to watch, though she
might watch light from lamps or static
from the cat. Winter doldrums near:
the sky is grey today, though leaves
burn through, yellow, red, and orange
(it's nice they don't turn black) and
flowers remain just flowers in front
of the neighbor's house. Gardening's
a pleasure as one "intensifies," my
word for growing older. The radio
announcer on the Javanese Gamelan
Show says the piece we're hearing
is called "Neglected Plants." How
utterly nutty of him. The instrument
resembles a truck breaking down on
a road; I imagine red and yellow like
those in Costa Rica with little canary

bells that jostle with the ride. Both
aggressive and coy, the dash of a
scarf on a wall, it sounds so engagingly
noisy, but the real attraction lies
in how many people play it, whole
villages consorting in the merry,
ugly music broad as the thought of
a mile. I have a look for thinking,
a mask of concentration that serves
as well as words, though words are OK,
too. Gosh, I mean, like gee!, their
glitzy mechanisms, the little springs
and whirrs of circling with outward
momentum the prey one self-creates.
Time is money (said). I have lots
of time. And there are lots of words,
even as topics narrow into single
"things," i.e., how you're feeling,
what didn't happen today, and more or
less how's the folks? The fog that
never lifted. The fever of trying
to mean when the slightest nod would
do—how noble is the speaker in his
very foolishness. Silence forever!
Prudence. Fueled by self-revulsion,
we practice our departure over cardboard
rocks and canvas-covered lakes, grimacing
with solutions in the midst of messes
made, for even the act of falling
is a generous exploration. (We land
in the room where we are with a knowledge
of all outdoors.) Last week I saw a
statue depicting Marsyas (who blew
from the flute such ravishing sounds
he was tempted to challenge Apollo)
in the midst of eating his beard,
in agonies of pretension. But the
crowd was more enthralled by a little
boy wrestling geese, a slight, libidinous

symbol of the kind that pees in fountains.
It was fun to walk around Calliope's
small breasts, an excavated muse.
(Uncover all of us later, and you'll
find us, hands in pockets, yawning
for all we're worth.) As for common
speech, how Marsyas must have cursed,
it's not just Nighttown slumming, but
rather the speaker's obsessions
cross-hatched in a pattern a long
black box with dials reveals as glyphs
on graphs. In the middle of all that
marble, I thought of my own nostalgia
for things that never happened, as
well as for things not said, how like
Marsyas I'd rather just eat my beard.
What's the way it is? Thelonious Monk,
with halts between the notes? A green
subliminal island? I'd like to say,
and rather directly, who cares about
that stuff? As for the matter of beauty,
I don't even know the names of flowers
beyond the dandelion—well, daisies,
violets, mums, carnations, gauche
birds of paradise, and phallic ambrosial
things Maxine sometimes buys to fill
the house with sex. But what's a gentian?
Forsythia's possibly yellow: that's
the end of it. Amaryllis, phlox, wisteria,
and bluet—I wouldn't know them from
blintzes, though I think I'm planting
gardenias when the sun lands on my hands
like that *Dark Victory* scene I watch
with maudlin tears every chance I get.
My mother in her thirties looked like
Bette Davis, except for the eyes, that is.
Now I'm off to bed. Goodnight, everyone.

5
What shall I think today? I can't
quote from Greek, don't know the names
of heroes whose weakness was their story.
But I know the work at hand, light touch
on the water, this broken-down typewriter
that can't even hold the margin. An instant
of the future slips into perception like
Dagwood's Mr. Dithers, and suddenly I
remember the honking of that horn
which I followed yesterday in a drunken,
empty rage and partly stupid bravado.
What if I caught the guy? Pound on
the roof of his car? Say, "Step out,
please, I want to scold you, sir"? One
mustn't act that way, so here's a solemn
vow that during the coming season I'll
keep my anger private and drink in
moderation. Today for lunch a burger,
French fries, and a Coke. Maxine, though
she's eaten, joins me for some talk:
how dull the mail has been, what Koren
is doing at school. Should we have
another child? Now there's a topic
from which to swerve like one drunk
chasing another, but the answer, in short,
is yes. Meanwhile, it's decided, I'm
Raskolnikov as played by Robert Young.
Now the alphabet: Ask anemone. Bob,
the better bowler. Cyanide in cases.
Delapidated dairy. Eagerness enlarged.
Fragments of two friezes. Goy, Italian
style. High-school hotfoot haven.
Ignatius the Inexact. Jacquette,
Illinois. The Klondike Kut-up Show.
Breath of licorice on the girl I used
to kiss. Memoirs memorized. Necking
with the sheriff. *Oranges and Orangs*
by Elroy Rutabaga. The perilous periwinkle.

Quinine sipped in Teaneck. Residuals
from the series. Study hall in silk,
or how Miss Simpson dressed. The tidal
decomposure, not decomposition (that is,
nervous excitement) of the beach beneath
the pier. A tireless tour of Tours.
Uncle's elevation. The virtual extinction
of everything I believed: swine among
the pearls. Whales that beach themselves
like satchels on a platform. A Xerox
of my head, whirlpool ear repellent.
"Yes" to what you whispered as we drove
into the night. Zero on the test.

6
I have found a brief wing should
too much of weight the felt have who
be need must there for Souls some pleased
if plot of ground scant song's within
bound be to time twas moods past day
me hence for is and selves a twist
doom price we gloves to firm this high
bells fox by hour fair hair strong ants

bells peak near night for track undone
bloom soar that sell a bee's bent dance
loom wheel weaves wheel at maids nor pure
sift here her pens their blood serves four
cells she her mitts which are content
invent their sheiks past at not at fret nuns

7
Paul Hoover was born on April 30,
1946, first wave of the baby boom,
to Robert David Hoover, a pietistic
preacher who'd cry at the sight of
Ike (his sympathy was with history,
any large event, not the man himself:
tears at a parade of only a kid and

a dog) and Opal Catherine Shinaberry
(altered from Schoenberg). The nuclear
family Hoover lived in the Midwest,
though their manner and sense of
tradition were actually those of the
South, with talk of sweet potatoes,
fried chicken, collards, and kale.
The feel of the wheel of the '49
Oldsmobile that drove the Hoovers
(formerly Hüber, farmer, umlaut over
"u") to church on Sunday morning after
baths on Saturday night. Thus time
efficiently and often sweetly passed.
A sampler on the wall contained a
smarmy prayer Flaubert would have loved,
not fleur-de-lis wallpaper but some
Dutch-uncle stuff: windmills, girls
in skirts, and oversized roses on a
blue background that seemed to breathe
in the night. Once, and only once,
was the radio ever played, and the
phonograph turned to rust, but TV
buzzed for days like flies in a corner
web. Young Hoover remembered sunlight
falling into the house, the eeking of
a screen, and sirens squeaking at noon,
not because of a fire, but just because
it was noon. In all of *Dr. Zhivago*,
the movie he saw twice, thinking it
high art, the chief thing that impressed
him was the thump of an iron on cloth.
He still had reason to wonder about
this young aesthete with the chic of
Field and Stream whose desire for
self-expression had the phobic width
of a billboard photograph, behind which,
he imagined, policemen started their
engines. The "self speech" of a tenor
who wants to sing Wagner like Verdi

instead of shouting it out like father
enraged at a candle. The absolute beauty
of a moist patch of grass on which glass
panels have fallen, which flattens it
to painting but still lets in the light.
(Be careful, by the way, where you step
in such conditions, for accidents usually
happen in or around the home, and even
a shoe too small can change the course
of a life. Pornography on ice, though at
first it sounds attractive, results in
nicks and burns. Aesthetically, too,
it hurts, as the grace of the skaters
collapses as other interests ensue.)
When Hoover went to a play, the pianist's
assistant, whose job was turning the pages
with the grace of a butler dancing, began
to quietly cry, moved by the show on stage.
As the music could not proceed, it turned
in quiet circles. Scenery fell on the
players as they scrambled to escape;
curtains went up when they shouldn't and
didn't come down when they should (painted
to look like bricks, they hung in folds
like curtains), and the amateur players
shrugged, as if to say, "So what did you
expect?" A joyous presentation, for they
preferred the mistaken, medium awkwardness
with which their acting moved. And then,
another time, the way three bulky dancers
careened in being swans, the creaking
of the floor beneath galumphing feet,
and a little old lady, whose black top
hat matched her tux and cane, doing a sly
soft-shoe in a mix of innocence and raw
determination. Young Hoover considered
it all, life's complexities as they
pertain to art and art's inanities as
they derange a life, and settled on a

manner of determined noncommitment.
Some day, he'd figure this out. For now,
he was satisfied that nothing holds
together, which in itself is charming.
He left in laughing tears. If things
were totally clear, like spreading
circles of light, not dim as candled
eggs where shadow shapes appear, his
constant indiscretions might cease
as excitations, though probably not really.

8
The tinny music clatters, Elizabeth
Schwarzkopf again. Was she the only
one singing fifty years ago? It's a
plodding, dying dirge more notable for
its age than for its lyrical pomp. Then
a cheery beer-hall romp with martial
implications: boys, let's go to war!
Today is Veteran's Day. Let the VFW
have it, baked bean dinner parties,
American Leigon bingo after white bread
snacks. An itchy ancient voice with
brassy coldness sings, "Pack up your
troubles in your old kit bag . . ."
That is, pioneers, wars will follow
depressions. So stick out your chests
with pride. It's life and all those
taxes for Rural Free Delivery and a
nuclear plant in your yard, glowing
phosphorent lettuce like poison left
out for the rats. But I digress from
the music which fades as the door
swings shut. Beauty should enfold me
in its cheap theatrical gown as a bat
enthralls a moth, but these are times
when several Marinettis spread like
stains on paper. Everyone wants to be
drums, sharp objects in the dark. It's

Berlin in the Eighties, and Warhol's doing
portraits for a little bit of money.
As John Singer Sargent said, the mouth's
where character's found: the sullen pout
and sensual purr or nervous hairline
fractures that mean you're disappearing.
The morbid hesitation when the person
being drawn sees himself as victim:
"It's quite, uh, lovely, I think" (knowing
he's been skewered). The wicked look on
the painter's face as he packs you off
to history, having caught your soul,
diminished as it is, but you'll look good
on the wall as the party swirls below:
"That man on the countess's arm, was he
not the janitor's son before his profile
saved him? And Klosterman's candy fortune,
which has started to melt away, is it not
maintained by the studio he keeps?"
Ordinary life offers the better pleasures,
as Billy Rococo said, dumping the ashes
of Rico the Tenor in a soggy Jersey alley
verging on a swamp. It had been a terrible
day, filled with incidents (murder) that
made him question his human position.
But what to do with Rico, whose mordancy
had sustained him yet finally wouldn't
serve? Down the alley, tin cans clattered,
probably a cat. The night was clear and
crisp. A leaf, in the act of falling,
swerved to brush his cheek. Yes, life
was great in Jersey. He breathed, in his
satisfaction, a micromilligram of
polyphenyl chloride, and a light went
off in his eye. "Billy," she had
moaned as he flicked her hardened
nipple with the tip of his throbbing
tongue and pressed her quivering hand
to the rising knob in his pants.

Great waves, friction, ardor, caresses,
stays, and snaps. Her warmth had now
enclosed him. It felt, it felt, so good!
"Rococo" was carefully written above
the front door bell of the house on
Paradise Parkway. "Welcome," said
the doormat. "Rico," he said to the box
containing Rico's ashes, "Rico, speak
to me!" But Rico's time had passed,
and now the wind blew down, scattering
everything into the swamp and beyond.

9
But let this make a world, as single
words can do: Sundays, Easter, Tuesdays
in Spring, Bank Holidays in Summer,
Christmas Day and Boxing Day, New
Year's, Easter Eve, and May Day.
Bill Atkins, Vincent Carter, Clifford
and Eddie Johnson, Art Hoyle, Danny
Barber, George Bean, Edwin Williams,
Bill Porter, Willie Pickens, Ron Kolber,
and Steve Barry. The Landslide.
The Condor. The Rescue of Robert.
The Open Sea. The Whale. Platform
and Ladder. Old Bad Money. Blureed.
River. Rooves. A Donkey Ride in the
Dunes. Glove, groin, fever, chimney.
Reading Perspectives in Poultry. Sunday,
Monday, Tuesday, Wednesday, Thursday,
Friday, Saturday, Sunday, Monday,
Tuesday, Wednesday. Diesel, feather,
clinger. Blond, backseat, drizzle.
Fetlock, padlock, thumbnail, mirror.
A slum. A cloud. A home. Closet,
crèche, recess, bowl. Why are fish
not given to fevers? Why are animals
soft in youth? What part of water
is more truly water, the bottom, top,

or middle? Why are fools so fond of
cheese? January, February, March,
April, May, June, July, August,
September, October, November, December.
Je suis le bon berger. Blanc comme
le neige. C'est moi qui vous console.
Man with tuba. Man in parade. The
giveaway, the false confession, a
mistletoe kiss on lips. "In answer
to your question, yes, I'm feeling
better, in spite of the fog in my
bones and dilapidated spirit like
soiled wallpaper. Things are clearly
improving for Bobby, me, and the dog,
but neighbors keep a standard of
ruthless censorship that makes the soul
feel soggy. Yours in penitence,
Prudence." So Puritans *do* lurk in
the almost modern conscience. We're
figures on a landscape sectioned by
strict hedges, which, even when they
flower, shuttle us off to a corner.
To put it another way:

        The Pilgrim's foot

dreamed a ladder

        May 16, 1950

Dear Grandmother

        how is the college

from all the guys

        to all the gods

Here's the train

        to Upper Tooting

failed designs

for a new triangle

hermetic signs

of a new melancholy

Mr. Swinburne

stalled in traffic

the glory of leaving

your pants unzipped

maliciously small

American music

egg-shaped marks

on flattened grass

the new magi

the new spoonbenders

Candy Bangs

Just Plain Beauty

antique seas

and modern water

schoolbells ring

and children sing it's

mother knows for

children's clothes it's

Jacob Epstein

William Blake

Nobody knows

the trouble I've seen

confusing aesthetic

with surgery

the dog that gnaws

on saxophones

J. D. McClatchy

teaching at Yale

whose final lecture

"Ballistics and Dancing"

when Amos Alonzo

was a verb

lyric filler

"satin and vacant"

a man of meat

a piece of dreams

Demosthenes

the letter "R"

shadows standing

in the shade

not for profit

Mendeleyev

the swarm contracts

round perfect trees

10

Dear Maxine: Thanks for sending
the magazine and book. Glad to have
them both. Wish I could reciprocate
with something new of my own. Enjoyed
meeting you. Remember many years ago

calling one time from Connolly's on
Devon (no longer Connolly's) to see
if you felt like coming out, but there
was no answer. Even enjoyed addressing
this to Jarvis. Used to call it Nervous
Jarvis when I lived there—13 something,
a courtyard building by alley. That's
another story. Hello to Paul. Best, Stuart.

Dear Stuart: Years ago, when you wrote
about Peter's book, I was angry with you.
How could you hate such beauty? Indeed,
I ask you now. For years I didn't write you,
but followed your career, resenting your
success. Now Peter has subsided, and we
stand as survivors, and while I still
defend him, I wish you the best and thanks.
Tonight we dine with friends whose policies
have changed from *succès de scandale* to
tradition, form, and craft. Afterwards,
a movie, something by Roger Corman as
cheap and overripe as our image of ourselves,
which gradually we're perfecting so others
may believe. My doubt shows on my face,
reversals and inversions that won't disguise
themselves, like gross banana slugs. But what
a nightmare thought! Joyce, I read today,
lived on Via Scusa. Does that mean Road
of Pardons? I hope you'll pardon me. Paul.

11

The lesser scoup is both a duck and a
sequence of events moving on the pond
where millions of water bugs are lurching
in circles like conjuring hands. Home runs
are events, dresses painted blue, and any
location, minus its wind, is there to be seen
if not to be hit. Its name is an event:
Grinder's Grove, Joe Island, Atlanta, Tantrum,

Gratis, and Reckless, Oklahoma. And then
there's Chagrin Falls: one wonders how
it happened. Some things never happen
but keep on happening: the weather,
how one talks, the attitudes of sharks
in warm or warmer water. And sentences
are events: "The cat sits on the mat"
and "Yeats, in search of a frame of character,
concerned himself a good deal with the dead
because their fundamental rhythms could be
determined." I put a ball on the table.
It is white and firm. It does not roll,
metaphors no moon, is not required of its
setting. Hostility from corners, snow
at the "anxious" window, for we often make
events where they refused to be, and in
a certain light we are events ourselves,
hogging center stage. When philosophers
go out to eat, we see how dizzy they get
watching milk descend from a pitcher to
the glass, accounting for its whiteness
by ignoring the darkness in it, where thousands
of events surpass their recognition. They
mark a point where the first drop lands
and build a shrine to it, while the last
drops away into what it is with such coercive
ease they think a thing has happened.

12

The work is fashioning, being fashioned
by the work—it sounds like "fastened,"
drunk. You've been depressed at noon,
pleased at two o'clock, run toward lights
of cars, slept in clean motels, mumbled
underground, done back flips from wedding
cakes where you were posed as groom.
The land is flat as you can stand, with
a dip in the road for a valley and rain
that shrugs toward coasts years and rivers

later. But a joy in your posession
insistently provokes like two within the
choir preferring other songs. It's a
meager tourist town where most of the
cabins are shuttered and paddle boats
are filled with snow no one could have
imagined under American heaven. Now they're
too heavy to move beside a quiet lake
frozen like a road, and the citizens,
whoever they are, must be sleeping in
for streets to be so empty at noon on a
winter Tuesday. Population: four. Only
your insistence might turn them out of doors
to pose for a picture together, but they
stay locked in smiles, inert anecdotes.
You might fashion them the way a child
draws mountains with blue chalk and some
haste, but they shake at your attentions
and even seem to say, "Please leave us
alone; kindly go away." Their world remains
itself, shaped like snow that falls on
rocks and walls without your intervention.

SIX POEMS

HUME CRONYN

PALESTROM HAS A DREAM

Palestrom dreams of a ladder in his head.
He climbs to the top and comes to a trap door.

At first it refuses to budge, then it swings open.
He enters into a room with a single window.

The walls are white. They turn red,
Then yellow, then waver with morning glories.

A tiger leaps at Palestrom, turns
Into a bird that sits on his shoulder.

A bare lightbulb hanging from its cord
Swings, and turns into a monkey, a child.

In the middle of the room, an apple,
It turns into an orange, a plum, a chair.

A girl sits in the chair, laughing,
She turns into a window, a candle.

Night plunges into the room,
A shark fin, scent of wisteria, daylight.

Palestrom sings; moons float from his mouth;
Fish swim through his veins.

Palestrom is at home in this room;
He turns into an owl, a birthday cake, a room.

PALESTROM TRAINS HIS BODY TO BREAK OUT IN THORNS

Palestrom hates louring after women,
Turning his head this way and that.
He hates lurking after them,
Hates the desire that persists into sleep.

Palestrom thinks it must be hard to be a woman.
How uncomfortable to be always stared at:
Must be like flies lighting on the face.
Palestrom hates causing so much discomfort.

So Palestrom, whenever he becomes desirous,
Has trained his body to break out in thorns.
And in the far corner of his garden,
He grows like the branch of a rose bush.

He grows and grows and grows,
Until towering, he reaches the clouds,
And the clouds wrap around him,
And caress his thorns until they are worn smooth.

And smoothed, he turns into a rose.
Then, how often he is picked by some woman—
To be worn in her hair, or placed in her bedroom,
Or planted in the warmth of her heart.

PALESTROM WANTS TO BE A TOILET

In a previous document, Palestrom revealed
The philological root of his name: PALEMAN.

Now he is having second thoughts about his name.
As much as he likes it,

There is one serious drawback to it:
People will think he is anemic.

The fact is: he is not anemic—
Only spiritually so.

He is constantly unsettled by the feeling
That he is the white walls of a lavatory—

Always seeing man reveal himself.
And the more that he sees,

The more he hates his role as a pale spectator.
He longs to play an active part—

He longs to be a toilet:
Not the cold aloofness of walls,

But the still water disturbed,
The act of flushing,

The deep embrace,
The return to still water.

Then Palestrom would no longer be PALEMAN,
He would take on the unadorned name of MAN.

PALESTROM REVERSES THE FALL OF THE RAIN

Palestrom loves the rain.
With the first drop knocking on his window,
He throws on his long winter coat,
And takes to the streets.

He thinks clouds are wandering eyes:
Eyes that see so much of suffering life
That they well up with tears
And cry and cry and cry.

Palestrom loves the rain.
It's a strange sort of comfort to know
He's not the only one who cries for man.
World and he are finally at one.

But sometimes he wonders if he likes the rain
Because so many others run to avoid it.
He likes the sense of weathering it alone,
And facing the world with wide open eyes.

But recently it has rained so much:
He feels that he is indulging himself,
And like the water streaming into the sewers,
He is letting himself be sucked away.

Once in a while, it is proper to be sad,
But other times, one must fight against it.
So Palestrom decided to reverse the rain.
He closed his eyes and ate an orange,

And with a great force of concentration,
He recomposed the orange in his stomach.
It lay there full and orange;
It lay there warm, and like a child.

And he thought upon this inward sun.
He thought and thought,

Usually they sleep in his feet,
They lie like icicles, so cold,
That Palestrom finds it necessary
To wear three pairs of socks.

But today they surge through his body,
Flick the warmth of fin and tail—
Whoosh, they fly and fling the spray.
God, does Palestrom feel good.

But Palestrom must go to the library—
He's a great believer in discipline.
No matter what the weather is,
He must do a few hours' work.

Damn his luck, Ol' Sourpuss sits beside him
—He has never said a word to Palestrom—
But today, he also has fish in his blood.
He leans across and whispers to Palestrom,

"This weather sure gives everyone a good flip."
And Palestrom sees all of London
With fish flipping through their veins.
How wonderful, thinks Palestrom,

Fish even live in this dead place.
But outside! It must be a teeming sea by now.
And Palestrom thanks Ol' Sourpuss,
And strolls out of the library.

Until suddenly, the rain . . .
It was flung back into the clouds.

PALESTROM UNLOVED

Palestrom always dresses in brown—
Boring, boring brown! Why not blue or red?

He always dresses in brown—
Shades of earth brown, shades of nondescript.

Today, he feels a little uncomfortable,
He's wearing a new shade of brown

—He feels like a chocolate bar—
But still, he will visit his girlfriend,

Sport his adventure into a new shade.
However, she fails to notice the change.

In fact, she fails to notice Palestrom at all.
Oh, why doesn't she have a sweet tooth?

PALESTROM FEELS GOOD

Palestrom feels great today,
The skies are blue and warm.
He skips through the streets.
No more winter coat!

No more bulky sweaters!
God, he feels transparent.
What does it matter?
Fish swim through his veins!

FREE FALL (R'S ACCOUNT)

ROBERT NICHOLS

1

. . . the experience was of falling. Not a fall in space endlessly and limitlessly. Like Lucifer falling through the light. One calls to mind the skydiver wheeling over and over arms outstretched the cold sunlight striking his nylon jumpsuit . . . Lucifer's creamy wings. Only sky and space. No earth rushing up to meet him (the earth has not yet been created, it was created by the fall). A timeless and boundless descent.

Not so in our case. The fall—or rather what I have to describe as the *experience* of the fall—was quick, abrupt, sickening, like a fall into a well through darkness. Darkness and speed. The walls of the well, clammy and restrictive—we are talking about a hole, like a hole in time—rushing by silently and at tremendous speed. Then we were through, and lying in a field.

I describe it: like a man who has fallen into a deep well and not only down but through. So that looking up into the space overhead (at the top of the sky, here there was a darker blue) we saw a small trap or shutter rapidly closing (an afterimage perhaps?) and beyond that, like a thin wafer, another sky.

I'm writing down a series of images merely . . . One speaks of the "vanishing blue sky"—that hue, that stratum, like some level of reality one has already traveled through in the past.

Or like (as over the water) a fish hawk or pelican. He floats, buoyant in his element. Then sheathes his wings, plummets, drops through the surface like a lead weight.

SPEED—WELL—FALLING—SUDDEN—AS-IF-THROUGH-THE-DARKNESS. THEN WE ARE THROUGH.
We are lying in a field.

* * *

There was the sudden collapse of the factory wall on top of us. I could hear J.'s scream—he was to the side at the far edge but carried down with us. This scream continued in my ears—I imagine in O.'s ears as well—through the descent. There was this scream and the sudden darkness which seemed to come out of it.

(I say "fallen," as if through the bottom of a well, but it was the scaffolding coming adown.)

It seemed as if ages of time had elapsed. But from the collapse of the wall and through the duration of O.'s scream—which came to us as a warning—it was only an instant.

The field was an open pasture full of weeds. I remember O. lying face down (still as death?) his arms thrown out among the thistles. Ahead of us was an enormous sunflower opening its eye.

Is this then the present?

An instant later? O. opening his eyes, getting up. His face pale, drained or washed clean—as if absolved from the past—he responds to everything freshly in the manner of a child.

2

We were walking through the village. An old woman had taken us on a tour of the place. Unfortunately the church, which is also the meeting house, was closed and the door shut. "It will open soon and you can go in," she told us with obvious pride in the building. O. was entranced with everything. He exclaimed, in an excess of enthusiasm, that we would like to visit this place again, the inhabitants had treated us well, given us a friendly welcome. Yes, we would like to come back someday, but probably we would not. There was not enough time.

"There is more time than life," the old woman said.

We were walking through the cemetery which lies right in front of the church. The town had been deserted during this hour (the hour of our tour). We were strolling along the gravel paths of the cemetery where, she told us, a number of her children and grandchildren were buried. On the graves flowers had been placed. "There is more time than life," she repeated.

She appeared to accept the fact with equanimity. It struck me how different her philosophy was from our own—whose life is composed of time, and when one uses it up there is nothing. The woman had the hardiness and good-humored serenity of the extremely old. She was absolutely plain (the picture of an American matriarch), even more, *solid*. There was a trace of Indian blood in her face.

The cemetery, dark with arborvitae, was bounded on one side by a high retaining wall, and beyond this was the town square reached by a flight of steps. On top of these sat some old men wearing picturesque and tattered uniforms—the uniform of the militia perhaps.

"But they are all dead," J. exclaimed, the phrase startling us. But he was not speaking of the men. He was referring to the graves among which we were passing.

* * *

We had been taken on our arrival to the old woman's house, no doubt because she was the principal person in this small town. Or it may have been for other reasons. Next to the house there was an herb garden with medicinal plants. These she pointed out to us routinely and without emphasis. Then we were sitting in a room with a brass bed, obviously the bedroom, but also the principal room in the house, the reception room. By this time people had come in to see us. I couldn't tell whether it was her large family or ordinary townsfolk. Among them were several older men whom I took to be her sons. One of them she referred to as "The Captain."

There was to be a ceremony of some kind. Perhaps we were to be healed. The old woman was obviously a healer. She had brought in bunches of herbs from the garden tucked in her apron. (They must have noticed we had arrived in some state of damage. Certainly dazed.) But instead we were treated to a good deal of light-hearted banter. The captain doled out to the three of us a shot of rum and took some himself.

"Obviously we have arrived," J. said.

The children had crowded on the bed and were looking at us with a delighted curiosity—particularly a little girl, who with her finger in her mouth, sat staring at O. The older folk treated us with a matter-of-fact courtesy, as if the occasion demanded ordinary politeness and no more. The three of us, with the old woman and the captain, were sitting in a circle of stools on the dirt floor. Heads turned as other people kept crowding in. There was an air of benign expectancy.

"I think there is going to be a formal greeting, an exchange of gifts. It is customary," J. said in a whisper to me, looking around. There were people standing with articles wrapped in cloth napkins. Then they presented us with some very pretty articles of folk art, while the captain made a fuddled speech.

"We had better give them something. They expect it," J. said with an air of a man who understands everything and who had been through it all before.

"But we have arrived with nothing."

I watched J. as he took out his wallet, looked through a number of articles, including some parking tickets and his identity card. He handed them, with some satisfaction, a dollar bill.

3

J. and I are both worried about O. He is obviously the worst case. In the blast his clothes were blown off. He had arrived on the field completely naked. The villagers had found something to cover him, a plaid shirt and rough woolen pants that someone must have had along extra. And at the village he has acquired a pair of shoes, much too large. He appears in the best health. It is not his physical condition that worries J.

"He was struck on the head as the wall fell, and suffered a concussion. He'll come round I imagine."

"Do you think he will?"

An amnesia victim.

Curious (at times it is amusing) that he has no recollection of who he is or how we got here. Though he recognizes us as his traveling companions—this is inconsistent. Consequently he has a mild open-eyed view of this world, the village, as if he himself had been born into it and had no personal history. This makes his responses to the natives guileless and fresh. (Another way of saying that he takes them at their face value.)

J. of course landed untouched. Neat and freshly shaved, in his usual trench coat and grey fedora. Strangely enough he *continues* freshly shaven, though we have been here almost a week. He complains that he has no change of underwear. "I would have brought something, a toothbrush . . . if I'd known this was going to happen."

My own injury is giving me some trouble. At first I didn't take it too seriously—a sprained ankle. I found I could walk . . . this while we were walking across the meadow toward these people who had found us. Still, there is a deep gash. J. tried to clean it out, and bandaged it with a strip of his shirt.

The wound keeps opening. I have spells of dizziness.

* * *

I've been having confusing dreams. We are approaching our destination by car . . . possibly it is a limousine. It's nighttime. We are at the crest of a high hill or range of mountains and speeding down. Below there is a band of hazy light, glimmering, a vast expanse stretching over the plain for miles, like a city seen from an airplane coming in to land. I am reminded of coming into Mexico City or Chicago. A kind of winking stratum, like a star galaxy seen from on edge. Then we are down, into it. We plunge through the film and it disappears. We find ourselves riding slowly under individual streetlights which glow on sidewalks.

I tell my companions this dream, the dream of arrival. "When we wake up in the morning it is not a city at all but a rustic village. The waking is part of the dream."

"What do you mean by rustic?" J. asks me sharply. "I suppose you mean homespun pants, cows in the street, etc.?"

There is something in the tone of the question that makes it impossible to answer. I realize he has misinterpreted the dream.

* * *

We are surprised to find the inhabitants of the village think they have rescued us from wild dogs. According to this version some children were out on an ordinary ramble through the meadow after blackberries. Or possibly looking for blackbirds, the language is unclear. They heard an enormous racket which frightened them and ran back to summon the others. Some older people went out armed with sticks and muskets. They approached shouting and firing the muskets in the air. And so had scared off the wild dogs —or wolves possibly—which were already upon us. (As evidence they point to my wound.) No doubt the villagers were busybodies and vigilantes probably, who had seen no animals only the travelers—and fired off the muskets to reassure themselves as much as anything else.

* * *

We were transported at night by truck, jammed into the back along with fertilizer sacks and crates of chickens. It was cold, we had on only light clothes. We held on to the rattling sides for dear life, slipping over the floorboards. One headlight was out, and the other barely penetrated the murk ahead. The road seemed to go up then down again suddenly in spurts. It was painful for me to be standing, the experience was extremely disorienting.

But the trip seemed to have revived O. Probably the cold air. Or it may have been the effect of having to brace himself against the sliding. His strength returned. As the truck came to a stop (we were at a bus station or in front of a large house or compound, there were people coming toward us) O. leaped to the ground and went to greet the advancing villagers with a broad smile.

The fact that (this happened last night) the driver and some of his cronies were comfortably in the cab of the truck warming themselves and swigging rum—and that we were forced to ride in the back in the cold—was offensive to J. He complained of it to me today and says he will lodge a complaint to the authorities.

"We're not on firm ground. We don't know these people."

"I know them only too well."

J. was insulted by the truckdrivers. And he tells me that he finds the local inhabitants primitive and "almost repulsive." They are simply peasants of an undeveloped type. And their lives (he quotes an authority) "will be nasty, brutish and short."

* * *

Again we were in the cemetery. We had been struck before by the character of the gravestones. J. wanted to examine them further. The two of us walked over the gravel path between the rows of graves. O. had wandered off someplace. The cemetery held no interest for him, obviously.

Jars of native flowers and little flags stood sentinel over the graves. The large plots divided from one another by a granite curb were the resting place for an entire family. The carving on the headstones was a dignified rudeness. J. was admiring them.

"The craftsmanship is very solid. They made them of slate or granite in those days so they would last. None of your smudgy limestone. And no sentimentality—that was to come later. With your weeping willows and drooping melancholy figures."

"Later?" I looked at him puzzled, wondering what he could have meant by the phrase, as there were no other graves than these. But J. had not heard the question and was bending down to scribble some notes.

"A particularly fine stone. I want to make some rubbings. I had the idea when we were here last, I should have brought paper and charcoal." And bending over this particular headstone he began taking measurements.

J. had not been at his work long when we heard a great commotion in the square. We had crossed it earlier, it had been full of noisy activity. It was both the marketplace and roadway through which traffic passed. A traffic jam had developed. Drivers were sounding their horns. The line of vehicles stretched back to the town limits.

"Look, there's a bus."

A bus had just managed to pull up in front of the hotel or tavern. It was covered with dust, but underneath it was a bluish color. Evidently the springs were not enough to hold up the large body, so that it tipped as the passengers came down out of it. From the roof two boys were handing down some goats.

J. had come up at my call. The same old men were sitting on the top steps. J. asked them which bus this was. In answer they mumbled something.

"And where is it going?" J. asked more loudly.

"To the next town." One could barely make this out.

"Well if it's going to the next town and if it's the only one out of here, then it's our bus!" J. turned to me in an agitated way and said we shouldn't waste more time. "We must find O. and make an effort to get out of here or else we shall miss our bus. I don't imagine it stops long."

4

Our bus hasn't gone yet, and apparently won't leave for a few days.

We have been given temporary lodgings in the hotel, actually the village inn or tavern. It seems to be also an old people's home. Among the residents there is a profusion of canes, arm slings, and ear trumpets. The wounds of life. Yesterday J. and I were sitting on the porch (O. had gone out) looking out on the square, as the old men smoked or chewed their quid of tobacco and spit over the railing.

The militia was drilling on the square, or what looked like the militia.

"I take it—as far as I can make out from the costumes, which are pretty ragged—that those are revolutionary veterans?" J. asked the question of an old man.

"That they are," the old man, evidently himself a veteran, answered proudly.

"They are from here?"

"That is our Hartford muster. And this is the town of Hartford.

"Hartford?" J. repeated the word after him. "That's quaint. As a matter of fact we are going to Hartford."

The old man gave him a queer look, as if he were a little daft, and scratched his beard.

"Well, I don't know. You're *in* Hartford."

* * *

Sitting on the veranda again today, again we were watching the recruits drilling. They were under the command of the captain. We recognized two of the recruits. They were the two boys who had been struggling to get the goats down from the top of the bus. They were now in a semblance of a uniform, which appeared to be shared out between them. Whereas on top of the bus disembarking the animals they had been agile, in the drill they were only clumsy, kept bumping into each other and knocking together their muskets.

Rocking in his chair the old man had been telling us the finer points of mustering. Dust rose from the square.

"I thought the word meant 'recruiting' in the old usage."

"Drilling? Is it the same as mustering?" J. remarked bemused.

"When they *appear* they muster," the old fellow explained. "Only these ain't appearing very well. But they'll get the hang of it."

"But what is all this for?" J. asks the old man, waving the dust away from his face. "Oh I know, the British are coming. But my dear man, they have already come."

* * *

Our bus hasn't left again today. It's being repaired, we are told.

"I expected as much," J. said, "when we first saw it."

The bus station is in the tavern—in fact it is from the serving counter that tickets are sold. No tickets are being sold, only beer and sausage and whatever odd scraps are dealt out to the old men. Consequently the bus station is full of flies. On the wall behind the counter is the bus schedule, a large ruled board. Crudely chalked up are the place-names and times of arrivals and departures. But it is so covered with dust and grime as to be almost indecipherable.

J. has been trying to get some help making out the schedule from the barmaid. Her sleeves rolled up, she is behind the counter wiping out beer mugs with a rag that is none too clean. She is paying little attention to J.

"I suspect, from the way you manage things here," he says annoyed, "that the bus station is closed and the line has gone bankrupt. And by the way you keep the schedule on the wall—under a film—you are trying to hide it.

"No sir, the wall is wiped every day. It's the soldiers that kick up all the dust."

It turns out that the captain is also the bus driver.

5

O. has fallen in love.

"With whom?" I ask him, astonished. We are taking a stroll through the village.

His sweetheart is a country wench, he's had an eye for her since the day of our arrival. She had been at the welcoming ceremony.

"What . . . At the old woman's house?"

"You saw her maybe . . ."

She is the old woman's granddaughter or niece, O. thinks. He has been going there every day and still hasn't got the family connections straightened out.

"What does the old woman say? You know we are leaving?" One talks to O. as if he were an irresponsible child.

O. won't hear anything about that. The idea that we are bound somewhere else, that we are in the village only temporarily, is beyond him. He knows only that he is here.

* * *

An instant ago O. was lying among the thistles his arms thrust out, the body twisted in a peculiar way. Looking at him I thought he was dead. It was the sprawl of the body more than anything, limp like a doll. His face chalk white, drained of blood. The next instant he sits up, rummages through his pockets for a pack of cigarettes.

He smokes, vomits.

J. tells him: "I don't think you should smoke. You've had a concussion."

My own head is spinning. I too have a feeling of nausea. Something barking in the sky. A flock of crows . . . like a squall rapidly darkening the water, like a tide rip. Beyond the field—I think it was at the edge, over the woods . . . a pali of smoke hung from a factory chimney.

OR

O. lay in a kind of swoon. As if dead? As if under an enchantment ready to break.

We are lying in the field. It is flat and mostly open where the cows have browsed. Patches of thistle. Ahead of us this enormous sunflower . . . beams on us its eye. Like the eye of a locomotive. Is this then the present?

O. sees everything between heartbeats.

* * *

J. has become suspicious and thinks of all sorts of reasons why the bus has not left. The fact that the bus driver is also the captain, and that the captain is the son of the old woman, the chief authority in the village, does not reassure him.

"But why? Why is it being delayed so long?" J. asks the captain.

The captain (who's been drinking again) gives a rather farfetched explanation: that something is wrong with the engine, it's broken and needs repairs. Or that it has been fixed already but they are waiting for a part to be delivered. Or that the road ahead is bad . . . the bridge is out, etc., etc.

"Well, I can't make him fix the bus," J. tells me irritably after the man has left. "And I didn't make up the schedules."

But all this seems to J. to be merely excuses. Could they be trying to keep us here for some reason? The idea is preposterous.

* * *

J. has developed an antiquarian's interest. Every day he takes his paper and charcoal to the graves, and rubs. The task requires skill. One mustn't press too hard or the paper is damaged; too light and one will not get a good print. Pleased with himself, J. seems to be more interested in his artifacts and copies than in the original.

Yet these are solid stones plainly cut. As J. says, there is no sentimentality here. The strokes deep in the blue-black slate or gray granite. One sees the cutter's firm hand in the work. Now the hand is gone. I remember the old woman's phrase: "There is more time than life."

However, moss or lichen cover many of the stones; the letter faint and illegible. These J. tries to pull out onto his copy, first scouring off the lichen.

J. rises stiffly, brushes the dirt from his knees, and with an armful of his rubbings crosses the town square toward the hotel, where he will put them on the wall of our room.

* * *

Listening to O. speak (he comes back each night to tell us what he has seen) I have this strange sense of oblivion—as if O.'s disease, the result of the head injury, has afflicted me as well. O. has forgotten who he is. Strangely enough this does not put him at a disadvantage here.

With me it is otherwise. When at some moment I sense the world we have come from slipping away—this occasionally happens—it is with an almost painful apprehension. It is not fear but being at the edge of fear. As if one's strength were ebbing away, like a swimmer who, bearings lost, is being pulled out by a tide.

J.'s theory is more reassuring: our experience here—the ceremonies at the old woman's house . . . the square where the militia is drilling . . . the bus that is continually departing and not departing—this state is purely mental. As if our reality—what he had called our "present"—had been wiped out by some invisible hand. If one could only shake one's head, or blink one's eyes hard, we could get it back.

Don't you see, they are trying to *prevent us from returning,*" J. insists. Meaning a return to consciousness.

* * *

O. and I have been going out together on long walks. O. is completely acquainted with the town, goes everywhere in it. He follows the cows down through the cobbled lanes to their watering trough every morning. A small boy follows behind with an alder switch. They often go by themselves as if they knew each lane well, or were being led along by their tinkling bells. The only place in the village O. does not go is the cemetery.

On our walk today O. takes me through the herb garden behind the old woman's house to the orchard. There are low-branching apple trees which stand in the mown hay. Running his hand over the bark of one of these (there is a swelling on the branch like a woman's breast) O. tells me that it is "tender."

Some memory of my own comes back to me—a childhood scene where every detail is clear and vivid—as if O.'s touching had brought it back.

"Tender!" I cry.

"Tender . . . and streaks of green. Yes, one can *see* more when one is in love."

6

The old woman's house is composed of many houses. These are all small compartments, separated but adjoining a common yard. Here there are geese, disposed to be ugly. The ganders hiss, beating their wings. One avoids them as one can.

Otherwise the large compound is a friendly but somewhat dilapidated place—as befits something standing through the generations. The houses are of modest proportions with dirt floors. At times when we have come we have been served meals out of several kitchens, perhaps by several different families or branches of families living there.

We have been to the compound more than once. J. wanted to see the captain. But he has not been in. For all we know he doesn't live here at all but in the tavern where he drinks and blusters. At other times he is on the drill field.

Today we have come and the place is deserted. We stand in the matriarch's room (the door is open). No sound from the adjacent kitchens, or even the barnyard. The room itself is absolutely empty. It's strange to think that we were once a curiosity surrounded by a crowd of people . . . and now we have become so routine as to be ignored.

I remember our first time; it was the day we arrived here. J., O., and I had stood in this room for the welcoming ceremony. We had been in the center on stools during the exchange of gifts.

Having presented them with his dollar bill, J. was looking at a plastic-covered card before putting it back in his wallet.

"But I have nothing to give," I said going through my own pockets.

"Better give them something."

"Maybe this will do." I found a photograph. J. glanced over my shoulder as I held it up. The snapshot was torn and faded: a couple with children in front of a house.

I said, trying to explain, "It is a picture of me when . . ." I held it toward her, as an offering. And the old woman reached out a gnarled hand.

Later, walking away from the house J. said to me, "I wouldn't have given her that if I were you. It's bad luck. You may regret it."

I was surprised at J.'s superstitiousness.

* * *

I've learned from O. that the villagers dislike J. But this is not surprising. His manner puts them off. There is something both tenacious and disconcerting. It's not that he's not interested—quite the opposite. He will hear a phrase or notice how some villager behaves or responds under certain circumstances. The notebook comes out. There follows a set of questions. But they are hectoring questions, as if from a privileged position and as if the answers are predetermined.

Or perhaps it is his grave rubbings that give offense. As I explained, he goes to the cemetery almost daily, choosing the hours when the church or town hall fronting the cemetery is closed. (I suppose it is during the lunch hour and there are no parishioners or office workers looking out the windows.) But still he is on full sight of the square. He can be seen on his knnes scraping off the moss and lichen from the graves and taking his measurements.

"But these are fresh graves," O. tells me.

* * *

The villagers came out to rescue us, thinking it was from wild dogs. Or wolves. (As evidence they point to the gash in my leg—which is absurd. In any case, J. had bandaged it.) They had been roused in haste by the children, who ran to the village to get the others because "they had seen something." Or "had heard something . . ."

And now the children stand behind, frightened, as the villagers come over the field singing hymns, brandishing their sticks, and shooting off their muskets.

What the children had taken to be barking was actually wild geese—or an immense flock of crows whose shadow covered the field, suddenly and darkly, as if someone had drawn down a blind.

* * *

There is this wall of the factory that keeps tumbling down. The wall, we had barely noticed it before . . . it was beside us, or rather over us, and we were walking along a steel scaffolding in the shadow of the wall . . . was suddenly as if the shadow had become a weight. A shape moving and threatening (like a huge wing). We looked up and there were cracks opening in the wall. I heard O. scream.

The wall of the factory keeps tumbling over and over. We fall through the darkness, like dropping through a tunnel.

. . . at the same time from far below . . . the field with its thistles . . . its dawn flush . . . was rushing up toward us.

7

Our bus is to leave soon. So we have been assured. We went today for a final talk with the old woman. The old woman's house is closer to our hotel than I thought, and the village smaller than I thought. The night we were taken there, after the rattling ride from the field and as the truck blundered its way around corners and through innumerable side streets—I had the mistaken impression that we were in some large city, an outlying slum perhaps. And had half expected to be greeted in a foreign language.

We approached the house today, with its thatched roofs, branches with sunny fruits hanging over the wall, the familiar clatter of voices within the compound. People were going in and out from the street (moving with us). The place is at the center of things.

J. had come determined on a confrontation. It was not hard to see he resented the influence of the old woman on our affairs—and felt in some way threatened by the captain. In fact we met the captain as we entered through the front gate. He was shoeless and pushing a bicycle through the narrow space. As we passed he merely gave us a curt nod and muttered he was leaving. The old woman made a half apology for him (as we sat down), explaining that he had been drinking and was in no condition to meet visitors.

"But I wanted to speak to him particularly," J. cried immediately, with his perpetual air of putting everyone else in the wrong. "That is why I came. But he is always avoiding me."

In fact we were here principally to discuss O. O. was already there. J. was a little put out by this. During the entire interview O. sat quietly on the bed holding his sweetheart's hand and gazing peacefully at J. as if he had not a care in the world.

The old woman was neither friendly nor unfriendly to J. She was as ever polite but intractable. I sense (knowing the pressure of J.'s errand) it would be easier to move a stone.

My companion informed her brusquely that O. could not join the militia. The idea seemed totally to outrage J. Not that he could be against the militia (he had been indiscrete on this point once before with the old veterans). Nor that he had anything against a young man joining it if he were so inclined. A patriotic duty . . . "But not O. Preposterous!"

"Well, he's strong and fit. He's not a weakling."

"Fit, yes. But not a resident of Hartford. So that he cannot be mustered."

The old woman gave us to understand that O. had not been drafted, he had volunteered. The captain was particularly keen on him.

"Out of the question," J. retorted. "I don't think he's a recruit the captain would welcome. It may not be *noticeable,* but he's been injured. He's not completely *there.*" J. illustrated this state of O.'s mind by putting his forefinger to his head and rotating it.

"Now, as to getting married . . ."

Again the old woman smiled at O. "He's not a child."

"He *is* a child, that's exactly what he is. I certainly wouldn't consider him—ah—emotionally responsible. As to the partner of this . . ." Here J. looked witheringly in the direction of O. and the girl. "In any case we are leaving tomorrow. I can tell you, we don't intend to leave without him," J. cried.

There was gabbling in the street. Looking out the window we could see a young woman driving a flock of geese. They belonged to the compound, apparently. Moments later she appeared. She gave us a brief curtsey and, flinging out her arms, went over to O. on the bed and embraced him.

Apparently we had made a mistake, and this was the young woman, not the other, who was our companion's fiancée.

She was introduced to us as Tanzy.

I could feel J.'s embarrassment. He apologized.

"Oh that's all right," Tanzy said, taking O.'s hand again and giving us a straightforward smile. "He's in love with all of us!"

During the interview the old woman's attitude toward us had been one of detachment. I thought she was not so much resisting J. as being inattentive to him, unconcerned by his complaints and nagging anxieties—like a river flowing between its banks is unconcerned with what goes on there. The old woman simply observed J. and myself. Her face betrayed nothing at all. Her hands rested on her lap—they were deeply wrinkled but strong. The face was impassive.

Leaving, J. told me that he thought "she had Indian blood in her, that accounts for her impenetrability."

8

I was sitting in the hotel room. O. was out. J. had left a short time before to check things out at the bus station.

I was surprised to hear a knock on the door. It swung open. The captain was standing before me.

He was without his uniform—in plain worsted trousers and jacket. But he wore his officer's cap—this was respectfully lifted —and a row of medals on his jacket.

"I'm alone as you can see. The others have gone out." I had thought it might be the chambermaid. We were not used to having callers. The remains of breakfast were on the table, but there was no rum. "Unfortunately I can't offer you anything," I told him. "But if you care to sit down . . ."

Evidently he was not in a drinking mood. His whole manner was sober.

There was a period of silence. After a while I said, "Well, we are going today. Finally."

"So you are."

"Well yes . . . so we are. As you know, there's been one delay after another."

"Oh you'll manage it, I expect."

Why then was I feeling so depressed? We were leaving Hartford. And the point was *to* leave Hartford, was it not? J.'s maps and schedules were spread out on the table. Perhaps this accounted for my depression. The mere presence, the fact of J.'s maps and J. constantly going over them (preparing himself for the journey) lay like a weight. Something in me balked. I had been wondering whether J. noticed my bleakness.

The captain stood awkwardly shifting his feet and scratching his head under the gold-braided cap. Whatever it was that bothered him, he was having difficulty communicating it. Perhaps he was calculating what to say and what not to say. When I had seen the captain before he had always been drunk or blustering in some way. I had not gotten a good impression of him. Still, I realized he had a certain claim on me. And that it might be the claim of friendship.

It occurred to me he'd come to bid me a friendly good-bye. Then I remembered he was the bus driver.

"You'll be going with us won't you? I suppose you must."

"I don't know about that," he said as he scratched his head. "Maybe and maybe not. It all depends."

He went on. "I saw your friend in the lobby. He's a queer one. At the ticket counter. Didn't see me though. I managed to get by . . . and sneak up the stairs." He gave me a sheepish grin.

His business was with me then? Again I was struck with his air of embarrassed cunning.

He had gone toward the wall and stood looking at J.'s grave rubbings. He now wore an air of reverent awe—with his hat tucked under his arm he looked slightly comical. The pictographs, so skillfully gathered by J., lined the wall. I remembered with apprehension what O. had said about these being fresh graves. If they *wanted* us to go . . . if their interest was to get us out of here, then why the delays?

His eye caught J.'s maps. Now he was leaning over the table, puzzling, shifting his feet. The militiaman's cap was on his head again.

There were the maps and schedules, the times were circled and the route heavily marked with a straight line.

"Hartford," he muttered.

In fact it was plainly marked. I asked: "Is that not the main road?"

"The main road it is, I suppose you'd call it that."

From the square there came a disturbing sound. Going to the window and rubbing off the dust, I looked out to see the militia drilling. There was a volley of musketry followed by a shrill camp-duty tune played on the fife and drum. I had listened to them several times over the past week sitting on the verandah with the old men. This one was called "The Wrecker's Daughter."

I turned back to the captain. Finally he said—as if his reluctance to speak had been overcome by the drum roll—finally he said bluntly, "I don't like that road."

"But what's wrong with that way? It's the main road, is it not, it's well traveled?"

I thought perhaps that considering the state of the bus there was too much of a climb or the road was out at this time of year, it was impassable or muddy.

It occurred to me to ask: "Is there another one?"

"There is another road. You'd be better off taking it."

He had come to persuade me.

ANA AND THE SEA

DAVID HUERTA

Translated from the Spanish by Maureen Ahearn

For just an instant there's a breach that shines,
a break where I see Ana's face peering out with a confused
    expression
between the curtains of that house above the Amalfi coast,
and then I say: This must be called "memory,"
reality's attempt to recoup itself in a substance
    burnt into some other page of the calendar,
some other place different now from the facts printed on brusque
    delicious memory,
this turning of Ana's body against the afternoon, between
    the sheets and smiling with that typical moisture on her
    adolescent lips,
that conversation, afterwards, in Rome, when she told me
how and who—but especially who, I spit on this
    memory and I detest myself—
how and who, that first time erased yet present in Ana's
    sadness when she watches me, when she used to look straight
    into my eyes
and there was her air of a hard, agile animal, a trace of plea
    and humiliation I didn't understand,

that's why I must add it all up and look closely at this thing
    that's coming back,

this thing I call a breach in the passing of time,
a continuity in the intermittent or the other way around
(I wouldn't know how to explain it and anyhow it must be very simple),
an instant when once again Ana puts her hand out into that rain
and laughs by my side—28 years older than she was, but what did it, what does it matter, I tell myself
I told myself, it's true, unless . . . a moment when
the summer shared hits me ever so slightly and mentally I say
all those words she used to hear with an air of delight or indifference,

that's why I have to think that all that meant something,
the unexplainable drawing near and falling away in the fervent afternoons and evenings, exhausted, two glasses of milk in hand,
still in bed, in the pleasant heat that invaded our room touching us with fine threads
then wrapping around us, while hearing the sea was another way of living with one's entire body that couple of weeks needlessly prolonged in Rome
(but why did it have to be that way, why?), in the filthly exasperating traffic
meeting in Piazza Navona and walks—I didn't like them but she loved them—
as far as Campo dei Fiori, to see the children with bewildering eyes and frugal ways,
and afterwards walking as far as the *vicolo* where I was living
turning on the radio, asking her what she wanted to drink,
looking at the ceiling without thinking of anything, anything at all, until she'd smile and we would try again, uselessly, to reach
a true flash of what had happened barely four to six days before
and she would move toward me skillfully, flexible, in her pure young ardor,
that's why I must think about her, remember her even though now everything's in order again
(because, of course, all that was disorder, an astounding upheaval of my widower's ways,

a peeling away of strange layers of habits to see something that
was blinding, saturating me),
even though she may have gone as easily as she came (where or
who did she come to? it wasn't to me, I know that),
even though Ana, with those big fresh eyes in that olive face,
may not be here may not return, and I look in the bottom of these
and other cups of aromatic tea searching for a piece of that
kind of
miracle that is loved denied, found again, lost, broken
evoked bitterly alone in memory
in the middle of this pain in my side, answering letters from my
remote and ancient sister, my cousins who are on the verge of
dying of pneumonia,
in the middle of all this that I write to distract myself—
to keep myself away from that breach and to exorcise it—
from what I'm
writing with a ferocious fear of apparently believing
that I was in love with that girl named Ana, when I know
that it's not possible, no, because then nothing would mean
anything,

not even this starting to think in the middle of the dark rains
in this Rome so disfigured and beautiful in her intimate
distance,
that I see from my solitary, almost abstract window,
not even these considerations about time that I should have
thrown into the wastepaper basket because they're not what
I should be saying—and telling myself—
not even that taste of vomit rising in my throat that makes me
think about all my possible deaths,
not even this profound loathing—that I feel is unfair and
excessive—when I see myself in the mirror
and I think about Ana, about her golden skin shining unbearably
above the sea at Amalfi.

FRISIAN HORSES

E.M. BEEKMAN

Among the first things he did when they modernized the farm was to nail the skull of a horse over the barn door. According to Saxon superstition, it kept evil away. It was discussed in the village café, but since it was not the head of a cow, they let it pass. A foreigner, after all. Werner Haver, a German who had spent the war years in a Japanese concentration camp in Java, married to a German woman who had worked for a fashion house in Paris. Her father had been a cavalry general who had insisted that Hitler used the wrong tactics against men like Patton, men who were victorious because they understood horses. When the plot against Hitler was betrayed, General Schmidt was arrested, tried, and executed by hanging him naked from a meathook.

Ilse proposed the idea of raising horses in Paris, after she was notified that, as sole heir, she would receive a sizable sum from Bonn as *Wiedergutmachungsgeld*, a financial retribution from the West German government for acts of atrocity against her family. Werner was working at the time for a consolidated news agency, translating Indonesian speeches and Dutch political declarations for the French press. His father was one among many Germans who had worked in the former colonial Indies for the Dutch government. He had been a botanist, a peaceful man, totally absorbed in his study of tropical vegetation, and with only one abiding passion: to find a blue hibiscus a seventeenth-century naturalist had written about, but which no one had ever seen. He had begotten an only child absent-mindedly, and was sometimes visibly embarrassed by this heir of his flesh and seed. The father died in a Japanese concentration camp after he withdrew into a lethargic apathy because of the filth, the inhumanity, and the greed around him. Uprooted from his world of plants he could not survive.

Ilse's proposal in Paris seemed appropriately absurd. They had discovered that Werner would never father children. Perhaps a fitting legacy from the camp years, he felt. Why not raise horses, Ilse had asked. They were better than people, beautiful, and sexy. After all, horses were in her blood. Neither of them wanted merely to dabble. It had to be worthwhile, a solid project, something that would demand of their lives more than mere existing.

They had no desire to breed Arabs, or varieties of the British Hunter type, or American Saddle Horses. But the Frisian was the kind of horse they could both admire. It was practical as a working horse, it had been strong enough to bear knights in full armor, and it was not a high-strung prima donna, but a solid mass of gleaming black muscle. The more they researched the matter the more convinced they became. The Frisian horse had been allowed to deteriorate, had been neglected, been tainted with inferior blood. Yet there was still enough character left in the genetic pool to rear it back to its former glory. Breed it back to a pure race, invigorate the line, ennoble it so it would once again be the black majestic champion of its green homeland. There was for Werner the added factor that the Frisian was the horse of the *Nibelungenlied*. Brunhilde had owned a stud farm on the coast of the North Sea, and the black Frisians had been the horses of heroes such as Siegfried and Dietrich. But by the nineteenth century their stock had been corrupted with Spanish, Italian, even Turkish blood, and they were only in demand as burial horses, their sable heads topped by black plumes. Horses of the night, of the North, horses of Saturn. Yet they were also voluptuous. When a stallion served a mare it was as if the night had muscled its lust into this fist of a horse, its long sable crest and tail roiling like a furious black sea. Ilse resolved they'd only breed Frisians.

Through the years Werner had to admit that she was better at it than he was. He painstakingly logged the bloodlines, traced the ancestry of the stallions and broodmares, noted the combinations of feed they tried, and carefully noted down the physical aspects they wanted either to eliminate or enhance. But it was Ilse who had the feel for horses, who felt close to them, worked well with them. As if she were kin.

It had not been easy to purify the stock, to breed out the ersatz blood and bring the line back to the noble race it had once been. After they had bought the farm and built the stables, it took months of scouting farmyards to find Sigert, a three-year-old stallion who combined two prime bloodlines from the best of Frisian stud farms around the turn of the century. He was working as a dray horse and was for show on holidays. Ilse and Werner could not be really sure that he was the right material until he had proven himself with two acceptable colts. Their gamble had paid off, and from then on they worked with scientific dedication at the art of besting nature. And when after several seasons a colt wobbled on stilts next to its dam, a colt as perfect as their control of its destiny could possibly make it, they both felt like creators admiring their work of art.

It had taken an enormous effort of time, money, and dedication. Ilse had free-lanced as a designer for a string of department stores, stealing ideas from Paris and New York and changing them just enough to prevent lawsuits but retaining enough of the general impression of the original to entice ordinary women. Werner had translated, written advertising copy, even fabricated nonbooks, until he hit the jackpot as a ghostwriter for illiterate executives who needed speeches for conventions, board meetings, and strategy sessions with the brass. They worked inhuman schedules, caring for the horses during the day—feeding, watering, and brushing them, cleaning the stalls, exercising them in the paddocks—while at night they labored illicitly, looking out of the window every so often into the huge night, searching for the lamp they always left on in the stables, silently honoring an old superstition that a light kept demons away from the animals. During the lost hours between midnight and dawn they'd go to sleep in the separate beds they had not remodeled. The beds were built into the wall of the living room, about two feet off the floor, and hidden behind doors as if they were closets. In the center of each of the four wooden doors, which could be latched from the inside, the shape of a diamond had been cut out that allowed a faint glimmer to ward off claustrophobia. The two bedsteads were built end to end, divided by a wooden partition which served as the footend of the one sleeping box and as the head of the other. To share the other one's bed one had to be invited, and Ilse was not very hospitable to her husband.

There were days when the flat green land drove him crazy, though even that would seem like a luxury. The horizon was everywhere. The green, the cutting edge of the sky, sharp like a razor, slicing off singularity such as a tree, a post, a cow, a horse, infidelity, even cutting down a man if need be.

Oddity, no matter how slight, was a form a heroism here. Such as the preacher who lived in their house during the previous century. A tall, slender man with large eyes which seemed able to hold all that drizzle that sopped up the green. The man had to preach twice on Sundays to a parish of one hundred souls. Had tried to inspire faces that were as indomitable as the drizzle, with tough eyes and horny hands that squeezed udders every day, the only soft thing that could be fondled without penalty. People who did not cry and never sang, except for a psalm. And even with a psalm their hesitant voices indicated that that too was close to heretical excess. The sensitivity of the shy minister shattered on their harsh orthodoxy, but they refused to accept his resignation, and he hung himself from the bedstead in the living room and was remembered for having scuffed up the paint with the heels of his shoes.

Another melancholy man had to proclaim the New Testament in this green suicide land of Old Testament vengeance. They would have burned him when they found out that he had slept with the farmhand in the same bedstead and had committed "foul uncleanliness" behind the closed doors of the bed, the two diamonds allowing a pale gray light to witness tenderness of male hands on male flesh. They would have burned him except that there was scarcely any wood to be found in this land that boasted of treeless forests. So they horsewhipped him out of the parish, and the farmhand married a unwanted imbecile and proved on her that he was able to produce as many offspring as any other animal in the fields.

Werner had bought the farm from an alcoholic descendant of this line of ministers. The man had brought his wife and two daughters there to escape the city during the war. To feed them better, he had said. To give them fresh air to breathe, since in the city they only inhaled death, hunger, and pestilence. He earned some sort of a living as a rogue lawyer, doing the dreary research and copying chores of the more respectable counselors. He had never finished his studies nor had he passed the bar. While his wife and daughters grew sleek and glossy on butter, cheese, fresh milk, and whole-wheat bread, the husband began to drink. First herb bitters and beer, but soon drinking his gin neat in the only café in the village of Hynder. At first the local folk admonished him in their laconic fashion, but when he didn't listen to them they'd buy him as many drinks as he wanted but no longer said a word to him. After the night when the man mistook one of his daughters for his wife, the women left and the husband needed to sell the property to pay for the divorce settlement. Werner got the house cheap because the village people silently agreed that the place was unlucky, but he paid a high price for the meadow land. There's never a curse on grass.

Werner let his eyes roam over the fields to give them some rest from black flanks and withers. The wind rippled through the paddocks and lent a motion to the grass that resembled the long swell of an ocean. This was sealand after all. The rich soil had been deposited by the North Sea, bottom land with only the terps as meager safety islands to flee to from the floods in spring and autumn.

After checking on the horses at night, he could sometimes see the beacon of the lighthouse on the island of Ameland across the Wadden Sea. When the wind was from the north he heard the sea slam against the dikes. Nor did it need to be dark to get that peculiar feeling of buoyancy, as if he were floating over his own land. When there was a scrubbed light, clean, malleable, though unbreakable like pliant glass. And when this verdant light came after the wind waves, the grass became algae, the sun wrestled with the clouds and wrung an aquarium luster over the land, and the cows flapped their flippers and looked doleful like dugongs, the sea cows from the Indies whose tears are a potent aphrodisiac. His Frisians shriveled, curled fiddlehead tails and notched their backs, and floated lazily along with the current as sea horses, their male bellies bloated with offspring.

After some time it seemed to Werner that they had deputized their living to the horses, particularly to the stud Sigert and the broodmare Selma. The feed for the animals was carefully selected and prepared, while their own meals were slapdash affairs of bread and tasteless modern food from cans. They groomed their charges with loving care. Ilse especially devoted herself to the looks of a horse as if she were preening and fitting the highest paid models for the fall fashion show. She could make the long black manes shine and sparkle as if she were combing threads of water and made the black tails shimmer like a peacock's. When Sigert trotted through the meadows and his strong body funneled a stream of air past his flanks, the tail lifted by the breeze, the horse looked like a jet comet shooting across an emerald sky. Its owners wore durable corduroy, with rubber boots or wooden clogs, and flannel shirts in winter. The animals were carefully exercised according to a scientific program, while their supervisors wore themselves out and dragged their weary bones to bed.

Ilse and Werner also had to supervise the mating. There often were problems, the mare not willing, the stallion too excited. They put a bit and bridle on Sigert to curb him from biting and tied a rope around each foreleg to restrain him. The mare was brought into the fenced-in meadow closest to the stables, and her hind legs were fettered. Werner tied a rope around Selma's tail so he could pull it aside, for only one single hair was sufficient to cut the stallion's member. Werner held Selma's head, trying to keep her from bucking and moving while Ilse escorted the stallion. When the stud horse mounted she often had to direct his huge member to the right place, the way a fireman has to wrestle with the heavy hose to aim it at the heart of the fire. Brief, brutal, potent, hammer sex. Then Sigert was led away to graze docilely in the adjoining meadow while Selma would wrest her head free and look back along her body as if wondering how she had been violated. Though the actual foaling was the realization of their hopes, it was the coupling that for both of them was the fulcrum of their labors. And Sigert had fulfilled his promise.

It occurred to Werner that after the violent scene he'd often stay outside for a while to look at his birds. He had been given a peahen by a friend and had added a peacock because he liked symmetry and hated to see anything go to waste. In the beginning he didn't have the time to care, but when another set came along it dawned on him that the birds were important. That he needed to see the extravagant fowl sit on a branch high in the scarce elms and poplars which formed a windbreak to shelter the house and outbuildings. And he'd wait patiently for the cock to spread his outrageous tail, and in the Protestant landscape it was a lavish prodigality, as if he had brought an iridescent fable from the tropics where he was born.

A family of barn owls had nestled in the huge barn which, in Frisian fashion, had been built as part of the house. The peahens also liked to roost there at night, flying in through a window in the loft he always left open. And when they began to see a return on their investment, Werner hired a hand to do most of the physical work, and with more time on his hands, he caught himself longing for sweet linden trees and sparrows taking dirt baths.

After yet another onslaught of sex, Werner said to Ilse that he'd prefer a virgin birth. Ilse looked at him and left to wash her hands. Werner saw no need to tell her that Pliny reported how mares once turned their vulvas to the north and were mounted by the wind Boreas. Without benefit of stallions. The next day he bought a Siamese. To go with the peacocks. And he watched the elegant, sleek cat with pleasure, particularly admiring the intense blue eyes in the fawn mask of its face. It was an independent animal, and it clearly preferred Werner's company. He fed the cat the heart of horses because the meat was cheap and full of nutrition, watched it lap the blood from the bowl. The color of the seal point's eyes did not match the Frisian sky. It was fiercer, less natural, more like the remote turquoise the Aztecs used for the mosaic skin of human skulls. The cat's voice matched that of the peacock and also sounded somewhat like the owl's. Three haunting cries, like children in pain. He called the cat Bandung, after the city where his father had lived. Ilse denied Bandung his beauty. Perhaps he was art to her husband, but she preferred the unbridled forces of nature.

With more money coming in from selling the colts, they could afford help, and the added amount of time they saw each other reminded them of their marriage. Ilse now clearly managed the stud farm, and Werner felt more and more that he was on her payroll. They began to drink again. Herb bitters at first. At night they often lay in their closets each with a bottle and a tulip glass, the doors open, watching the television against the opposite wall of the room. During the winters they drank gin and stayed near the large open hearth which they had restored and where more than two dozen hams could be smoked at a time. In the cold evenings, after the last tour of the stables, they came back to the big fire, also turned the heat up, and drank. Heated on the inside and out, controls lapsed, and though this should have proposed closer intimacy, it frequently meant that they took their clothes off in the blazing room, and, though naked, maintained an invisible perimeter which locked out the other. Werner hated to have her hands on him, and Ilse refused to lie beneath him. He'd chase her around the room lit only by the fire, while Bandung watched from the top of the bed doors, his eyes red from the flames. She'd laugh when he slapped her rump or when he reigned her in by her long brown hair.

Ilse's body had profited from the physical labor. Right under a deceptive softness was a hard, muscled body, and he knew that if it came to a fight he'd better not show any scruples. She might tempt him with her arched back turned to him while she looked back along her side with a smile. But it was usually Ilse who mounted him, locking his thighs with her strong legs and riding herself to completion. And when she lay back he'd look down on her lithe body evaporating the perspiration on a skin the color of the wood embers, and she'd open her eyes and look him over, telling him that the typewriter was making him soft and he wanted to whip the general's daughter.

Ilse knew enough not to push Werner too far, but she made it clear that she disliked his silence and his curt, though polite, manner. She told him to grow his hair longer, but he refused to get rid of his crewcut. She mocked his family, the father who had loved plants and the mother who translated Javanese poetry. Such parents were no longer German. She remembered her own father as a man who smelled of leather, tobacco, and horse sweat, and who had, after all, been murdered and had not died from grief.

But she also remembered the afternoon when Sigert had broken loose from Werner's grip and had asserted himself. Ilse had yelled that he couldn't even hang on to a horse. Werner knew that Sigert had to be taught a lesson, that the horse could never be allowed to detect even the slightest wavering on his part, but when he struggled with the animal something else was added. The horse had bolted from the stables and was cornered in the yard. Werner lunged for the reins which hung down from the bit. With one hand and his full weight dragging the stallion's head down, he grabbed with his left a broom that he had tossed against the wooden fence. Behind him the mares neighed and whinnied. Sigert towered over him roaring and kicking, foam lathering his black muzzle. Werner was being dragged along, and he tried to dig in the heels of his wooden clogs to find a point where he could pull back hard on the animal. He knew that he couldn't let go. The leather cut into the palm of his hand, and the animal felt the man let up a bit and, taking the advantage, wheeled and slammed his opponent against the fence. Werner felt a rib crack, and he sagged somewhat. Sigert came down hard, one hoof splitting Werner's left clog, numbing the foot with pain. To get his balance back the stallion stumbled and slipped a little, his equilibrium still off due to the man hanging from his head. But it was enough for Werner to straighten up and wrench the head down. He began yelling at Sigert, remembered the broom and began to hit the horse on the neck until the handle broke. He pulled the head down further while the massive body pressed him against the fence, and he shouted at the black face and spit at it while the slobber of the horse blinded him, but he did not relent. A few moments later Sigert relinquished and stood still, his head forced down on his chest. Werner wrapped the reins around his left hand and walked the horse back into the stables.

He limped for weeks and had trouble breathing. He was taped from his waist up to his chest. It felt as if he had a leather vest on that was strapped tightly around his torso. With his shirt over it, it reminded Ilse of the girdle her father had worn for most of his life after he had been tossed by a horse and had dislocated his back.

That morning Werner had stood next to the private investigator, leaning on the railing of the parking lot, staring at the North Sea. Hundreds of white swans were bobbing along the dike on the land side. Behind them cars and trucks went by on the four-lane highway on top of the dike which kept the sea from flooding Frisia and Holland while providing the nation with a chance to add to its territory by draining rich grassland from the sea. The investigator had verified what his client had guessed. Werner had not said anything but was trying to count the numerous royal birds which seemed out of place on the choppy salt water. He had given the investigator his check, and because the man misinterpreted Werner's silence as grief, he had thought to reassure his employer by telling him that the wife of the lawyer Ilse was betraying him with had three children, all by artificial insemination. It was so fitting that Werner almost burst out laughing, but he had nodded to the man and driven back down the enormous dike to Frisia.

He parked his car at some distance from his house on a road that was higher than the meadow land it skirted. He looked at some wading birds feeding along a ditch: rails with their narrow bodies and long toes, squawking their harsh cry, and oyster catchers with thin, curved, red beaks like the tongue of an anteater. Watching the birds steadied him. He looked at the house and the stables on the slight rise of the terp. An artificial island in the green space where they once fled from the force of the sea. A mount of earth sloping from the prone body of the land, with a thatch of trees hiding the house as if it kept a secret, concealing something obscene. From either side of the shaggy mount flowed two ditches like two legs spread out with green stockings of duckweed.

He waited till winter, until the greater part of the day was an extension of the night. People stayed home, keeping out of the raw wind and chill drizzle. After the first weeks of hard frost, Werner put a ladder against the barn, climbed up, and took down the horse skull and tossed it on a pile of manure. Mistbanks overwhelmed the land from the sea. Gulls wheeled further inland in search of food, yet Bandung still followed him when he went out for air. He saw the lighthouse more often, and the lamp in the stables was lit earlier because it had to bring consolation for longer hours.

After Ilse had drunk too much gin one night and lay snoring in front of the open hearth, Werner strangled her with a riding crop. He went over to the stables and tied Sigert's hindlegs to a post on either side of the box's planking. He put a curbbit in the stallion's mouth and slipped a head-stall over its head. He spread a blanket over its back and went back to the house with a wheelbarrow. He carted the nude body to the stables and threw it on the horse. It took considerable trouble to lash it in the position of a rider. He finally managed to keep it upright by tying the long hair to the long tail and steadied it in front with a rope around the chest tied to the bit.

When he lit the house and had smashed the stable lamp in a pool of kerosene, he took Bandung outside and waited until the peacocks had fled for safety. Then he drenched the horse with kerosene and lit the long mane and tail. It ran off into a space that was no longer green. Of the lit horse he saw only two crests of flame showering sparks as if the night was shedding stars. The Siamese accompanied him for a short while and then left him alone in the dark. The last he saw were the eyes, reflecting a russet glow. Werner walked on in the direction of the lighthouse and hoped to reach the sea before the horse would. He wanted to see it extinguish itself in the cold, gray sea of winter.

TEN POEMS

ROBERT JUARROZ

Translated from the Spanish by Louis M. Bourne

TRANSLATOR'S NOTE. *The poetry of Roberto Juarroz distills the human experience of man's situation as a divided self, plagued by the dualities of existence, hovering between life and death. The introductory motto of his first collection, "To go up is no more than a little shorter or longer than to go down," illustrates his debt to Heraclitus, and his style maintains the pre-Socratic freshness of philosophy as inchoate idea with lyric roots. The untitled, numbered poems of the seven collections comprising what Juarroz calls "vertical poetry" form the many facets of a single gem illustrating the heights and depths of a journey toward recognition and self-knowledge.*

A specialist in library and information sciences, Roberto Juarroz was born in Coronel Dorrego, Buenos Aires Province, Argentina, in 1925. He took a degree in liberal arts from the University of Buenos Aires and continued his studies at the Sorbonne. He later became titular professor and director of the Department of Library Science and Documentation for the Liberal Arts Faculty of the University of Buenos Aires, director of the Audiovisual Course of Library Science for Latin America, and an advisor to UNESCO and the Organization of American States. In 1981 he was a special guest at the Second Congress of Spanish Language Writers in Caracas, Venezuela, and the following year was an honorary guest at the Sixth World Congress of Poets held in Madrid, Spain.

His first book, Poesía vertical *("Vertical Poetry," 1958) appeared in Buenos Aires and was followed by* Segunda poesía vertical *("Second Book of Vertical Poetry," 1963) and successively numbered collections with the same generic title in 1965, 1969, and 1974. The* Sixth Book *came out in his collected poems,* Poesía vertical (1958–1975) *("Vertical Poetry 1958–1975," 1976) published in Caracas. The translations appearing here come from* Séptima poesía vertical *("Seventh Book of Vertical Poetry," 1982). Anthologies of his work have appeared in Barcelona and Buenos Aires, and W. S. Merwin did a brief bilingual anthology for Kayak Books,* Vertical Poetry *(1977). Anthologies in French translation came out in 1967 and 1980. Juarroz has published one prose work,* Poesía y creación: Diálogos con Guillermo Boido *("Poetry and Creation: Dialogues with Guillermo Boido," 1980). From 1958 to 1965, he edited the literary magazine* Poesía-Poesía *("Poetry-Poetry"), and for a period did book reviews for the newspaper* La Gaceta *(Tucumán) and film critiques for* Esto Es *(Buenos Aires). He was awarded the Grand Prize of the Argentine Poetry Foundation in 1977.*

At the heart of Juarroz's poetry is paradoxical statement, reflecting the dynamics of being where extremes meet, where reality is recognized by the presence of its negation. An awareness of absence, not that found in the Symbolist seclusion of Mallarmé but a metaphysical wound, a feeling for what is not in what is, plays an important role in Juarroz's lyric concerns. With sometimes intentionally bare language and the subverted logic of a syllogism with untoward deductions, Juarroz deals with his major themes in terms of their precarious existence and denial: the look that dispossesses itself, the word that remains unspoken in its space of silence, the uncertainty of god with a small "g," the search of thought for a body to contain it in its growing oblivion, and the sense of life as a changing station on the threshold of extinction where one cannot remember or forget. Octavio Paz has called Roberto Juarroz "a great poet of absolute instants," and he becomes so in his capacity to share, in the "blind spiral" of hope, the solitude of man with all its moral implications.

TO USE YOUR OWN HAND AS A PILLOW

To use your own hand as a pillow.
The sky does it with its clouds,
The earth with its clods
And the falling tree
With its own foliage.

Only thus can the song
Without distance be heard,
The song that doesn't go in the ear
Because it is already there,
The one song never repeated.

Every man needs
A song with no translation.

TO TRANSPLANT MEMORIES

To transplant memories
From one man to other men,
As a grapevine is transplanted
From one terrain to another.
Perhaps this way you could start
Another kind of greeting and recognition
To replace these absurd gestures
That rarefy the air.

And if man could transplant his memories
Outside of men
Or graft them onto a tree or a rock
Or maybe onto the relative silence
Waiting between certain columns,
Perhaps another kind of meaning could begin
Instead of these poor maneuverings of wrecks
With which we explain nothing,
Not even absence.

If man could transplant his memories,
Death would not exist.
And dreams and madness
Would not be needed either.
Nor even love.

A BROKEN POEM

A broken poem
Like a trunk split by a lightning bolt,
Like a stem snapped
By the very frenzy of the flower it sustains,
Suddenly shows at the site of the break
Something that seems like a return.

The shame of loving only the many
Starts to turn love into madness,
Into a sun that shifts unexpectedly
To the path in front.

The poem breaks down
For love to recognize in its own substance
The oneness of the many
And lose its shame.

The poem breaks down
For the sun to return.

FROM THE BOTTOM OF EVERYTHING

From the bottom of everything
Springs the voice of a bell.
It does not serve to call to church,
Nor to herald spring,

Nor to mourn a dead man.
It only serves to ring
As a man would do
With his eyes open
If he were a bell.
It only serves
To surround lost birds
With a more resonant air.
It only serves
To make the song
That goes nowhere live.

A simple bell
That rings from below
Like a natural movement,
With no one to stir it,
With no one to hear it,
As if the depths of everything
Were nothing more
Than the selfless tolling of a bell.

TIME IS A WAY

Time is a way
Eternity has of watching over us.
We are the hybrid children of both.
And though eternity has other ways of caring for us,
Time is perhaps its most charitable manner.
Another way, for example, is death.
And yet another is sleep.

And there ought to be still others:
The imagination of eternity is boundless.
So, it would be no surprise that sometimes,
To take doubly good care of us,
Eternity would assume the shape of itself.

THE INNOCENCE OF LIGHT

The innocence of light
Is no good for the middling regions
And even less
For the foundations
And fingerings of the void.

Light cannot mold time,
But only muddle its traces
And tediously classify its shores.

Light is no good for seeing you,
But only for dazzling myself
And making me spell your false names.

Light is no good for seeing myself
But only for sinking my eyes
Into another form of blindness.

Light shall only be good for us
When, like a god,
It loses
Its innocence.

THE INCALCULABLE AGE OF GRIEF

The incalculable age of grief
Explains the insight
With which it found its creature.
It is like a text written
On the finest and most absorbent paper,
A text that devours the paper
And itself.

The insight of grief
Has made it find its preferred substance:
Man, who toys with resistance,
The only creature
Who delays the flower of his agony.

THERE ARE GESTURES THAT KEEP SLOWLY TAKING SHAPE

There are gestures that keep slowly taking shape,
Like peaceful organisms
Whose space should age along with them.
Thus occasionally, for example, the gesture of suicide.
Its itinerary has tried out
A myriad of other gestures,
Checking the different angles of light
As if they were imaginary stopovers
On a trip towards shadow.
Its form has previously suffered
Caress and blow,
The shiver of winter
And the dread of offerance.
Its larval exercise
Has already been at the source
And has used the most hidden line
Of all life's motions.

Yes. There are gestures that slowly take shape
And suddenly break,
Perhaps so the rupture
Can be doubled
And in full force may be found
The unlikely law,
The law of abandonment.

In any case,
Every gesture is a circle.
And inside there is always somebody dying.

WORDS JAM

Words jam
Like the worn-out gears of clockwork.
Loneliness slowly leaks.
And besides future,
The time of death is now also past.

I ought to start keeping an eye on certain areas
That are neither life nor death,
Nor lofty temperatures, nor kneeling climes.
I ought to start keeping an eye on my own neat ways.

It is true that I have freed myself at least
Of the illusion of doing without the props.
Even the rose needs a stem
and even the air a shadow.

Maybe once more I shall humbly have to
Dust off some forgotten aids
Or between eye and finger perhaps allow
The most intimate space
To gather again:
The perfect and visceral touch of a tear.

EVERY SILENCE IS A MAGIC SPACE

Every silence is a magic space,
With a hidden rite

The matrix of a word that summons
And a fundamental detail of antisilence.

The hidden rite can be, for example,
A death in winter,
The word in embryo
Can be simply the word "oblivion"
And the detail of antisilence
Can be the thud of some clods against the earth.

Or the rite, the vibration of tenderness in the night,
The word, a proper name choking itself,
And the essential detail of antisilence
A trickle of water slipping away on the dream of the world.

Or the rite can be the loneliness of a poem,
The word, the sign each poem conceals,
And the verge of antisilence
The sound of the hand calling inside the poem.

Silence is a temple
That needs no god.

FOUR POEMS

DOUGLASS WENRICH

TO

a young man embracing
nothing when he has nothing
to say (viewing man's maneuvers

as ape-like through trees
not slick along concrete

in some honey of a metallic blue
imported sports car blaring out

some loose definition
of music he has to believe

to be art,
notice the glide from limb to limb
the arc   cutting   the air.

THE BRIDGE

Two lean against the severe
border of stone. Through Halloween pitch
desires and a point of orange.
All clear.

Masks drop
at the feet of the enchanted.
In some other light sequins
dazzle those unaccustomed

to heights. In smoke, shaking
ice against glass. Resentless,
receptive to the spirit
swirling their minds.

To feel themselves
as though the other. A stillness
touching brings. Between them
the grinning shine.

RECOGNIZING A PEACH

Lovers and the newly married exist
in the words of a poet
like real life. One peach

being on a kitchen table, say,
a table coated with speckled gray
Formica, lit by the hated
fluorescent overhead.

Ah, those in love
devour the pulp and scrap
the stone the poet
envisions
dead center.

DOUGLASS WENRICH

LEMONADE BLUES

For one reason or another
love breaks on a sidewalk
like a glass in final clarity.

At the feet of the disenchanted
pieces are never one again.

No matter how put together
the form will be

something else. Bitterness
taints what can't be

swallowed. Imagine a moldy lemon
as the predominant flavor
in an almost empty decantor.

THE TRULY GREAT STRIKES WHEREVER IT WANTS

LARS GUSTAFSSON

Translated from the Swedish by John Weinstock

He came from one of the small farms high up toward the forest; strange things come from there occasionally.

Sloping meadow barns, sometimes with a crack in the ridge of the roof right at the middle, small cowsheds of cinderblock, which cannot be used anymore, since the milk trucks have become too large for the small roads. And the road into the forest like a green arch. He played between cowshed and house as a boy and was always forbidden to go behind the cowshed and into the forest.

It was a marshy forest, mushrooms of all sorts, a place with abundant species, as can sometimes be the case where there is a lot of shade and various kinds of rock mingle.

It was quite a small place; he had two siblings who were older, by two and three years, a brother and a sister.

His first school was a woodshed; his brother and sister were often there, whittling their boats and cars. They were practicing with tools. He himself was afraid of them, maybe after some unsuccessful early attempts, afraid of the chisel's sharp edges, which could cut into a fingernail like a knife into butter, the hatchets and the large axes with their shiny shafts, and worst of all the saws that hung in a long row on their nails, all the way from the large lumberman's two-handed saws with their bows and clasps to the one-man crosscut saws, the joiner's saws with their buckle pegs that made a funny clatter when you released the tension, the one-man crosscut saws that oddly enough were called "tails" even though they didn't have the least thing to do with tails—grownups found so many strange names for their things, it was their peculiarity, and they had a *right* to all these names, a right he didn't have. He always laughed awkwardly and went off into a corner when his brother and sister tried to teach him the names.

It was their business: dovetail saws, punches. The old wooden club that was used to pound in fence poles, made of curly-grained birch, battered by tens of thousands of blows of wood against wood, impossible to pull up. And above all, hanging majestically: the ice saw, absolutely forbidden to take it down, a fierce giant with dragon's teeth, an enlargement of all the other saws, fiercer than them, but also silent, expectant, never used.

He could dream about all the saws' teeth.

He got smacked occasionally, nothing dangerous, but smacked anyhow, when he came from the woodshed with a wound and a gaping gash from the tools in the woodshed. They were afraid that he would really hurt himself. They wanted to keep him away from the tools. His brother and sister were allowed to handle the tools; they knew how. That made him feel that words belonged to them too.

Sometimes they played ridiculous tricks on him, too. They sent him to get things that didn't exist, an "eyeball" and the like. It gave him the feeling that it would always be vague and uncertain as to which things existed in the world and which did not. Clearly the use of words was more difficult than you could imagine. They always laughed out loud, doubled over from laughter, when he returned empty-handed, or when they had coaxed him all the way into the cowshed hunting for nonexistent objects.

In reality only the strong ones decided what words would be used for.

Mushrooms were better. They didn't care about having names. They had smells instead, smells of rotting leaves, of heated iron, of oxidized copper, some like rotting animals and some with mysterious smells which don't exist elsewhere.

And the shapes, most of them round, but all in different ways; some with a hollow in the middle, as if the whole thing had rotated around the middle at great speed once and then stiffened, some with indentations, wave-shapes, some with tall narrow stems, some with a cuff, some with finely placed gills under the cap, so fragile that they crumbled at the slightest touch. And some with an organ of fine pipes.

Occasionally covered with slime, which made you pull your hand back quickly, occasionally dry, brown, friendly to the fingers, as if they had attracted the sunshine and still preserved it as a mysterious force under the skin.

And then these remarkable things that came late in the autumn, which smelled like mushrooms and yet didn't look like mushrooms but something else: a little red finger that gropes its way up between two rocks, a strange hard lump, sort of like a pat of butter molded into a lingonberry-leaf shape, something indescribably gray that ferments and grows and turns around in the cracks of a rotted tree trunk. He felt an identity, a friendship between himself and these fresh things without names that changed day after day and soon disappeared again like vague lumps of decomposing life in the moss.

He thought it was worse to be forbidden to go to the mushrooms than the tools.

The autumn he became seven and was supposed to begin school turned into a catastrophe.

It was a little school, down by the lake, a single teacher, a single classroom, and the teacher a little broad man with gold-rimmed glasses and strong short hands.

A decade later he still remembered favorably the teacher's broad strong fingernails. They looked like those objects that really exist. He was supposed to learn to read, and the teacher was friendly and helpful, sat for a long time on a chair beside him, smelling of strange smells, tobacco and palm-oil soap.

The letters were easy to keep apart, but he never got any words out of them. They didn't want to talk.

That wasn't so odd. He didn't have any words to set up against them, nothing to meet them with. Nothing at all. He tried to copy them, and they turned into mushrooms.

It was natural that he went around by himself during recess, poked in the grass with a stick, while his brother and sister played with their schoolmates.

There was nothing that wasn't obvious; and he just couldn't understand what there was for him to do in school. There was noise. It bothered him to hear so many children laugh and shout to each other all at once. He longed to go home. When it got to be afternoon a wind came through the large ash trees outside the schoolhouse.

The trees are so happy, he thought, when the wind comes. Then they have something to do.

He was really at school for only a week.

What he later remembered of it was that it was at that place where for the first time he noticed a smell he would become familiar with later on: the smell of cleanser and disinfectant, the smell of clinics, the smell of the waiting room of the county medical officer, strong in certain places and weaker in others, but always the same, varying in one way or another: *the smell of those who wanted something from him.*

The lunch music and the voices on the radio. The voices on the radio became important for him later on; they confirmed that he still existed, they hovered around him, especially at noon, cheerful, persuasive occasionally, voices that filled the air, music that filled the air and didn't want anything from him. It was later. When they had come and taken him.

They came and took him one afternoon that fall; his parents clearly in agreement, his mother along in fine dress with a travel bag of paper tied with a cord (he was to see it again time after time over a couple of decades, it finally became one with his mother), an emergency taxi with a low-voiced rumbling producer-gas engine at the rear, roads and carsick throwing up in to the city.

Then the House, large, white, behind trees and fences. And the smell of those who wanted something from him.

Entirely new smells. The aides in their uniforms with high collars and maternal aprons, often somewhat older, round, sturdy women had another smell. The food smelled different, was different, mealy, gravylike, floating around, more watery than at home in the forest.

And was eaten in a common dining room during a frightful rattling and spilling. Some of his new schoolmates had trouble handling spoons. Some of them let the food run out the corners of their mouths.

He was afraid of them.

They didn't do anything to him. Most of them moved slowly, some were so deep in their own worlds that nothing would have been able to disturb them. Language was so distant from them—the "other's" language—that they had nothing to quarrel about. They were in the same living space, and the food sufficed for everyone. The food was important: it was a maternal emanation, a welcoming aroma, a connection with the other world that wasn't something forbidden. That took time to discover.

The first autumn he was too paralyzed to notice anything like that. He still missed his own world, the woodshed, his mushrooms, the smell of milk that while still warm was strained in the cowshed, the pigs' funny wet snouts, the ever muddy laces on top of his father's boots that swung around the bootlegs in perfect time when he walked out in the morning.

He missed a world.

Under the bed he found a spider he used to play with in silence in the evenings, until one evening he happened to pick it apart leg by leg.

He was too interested in seeing how it was made.

The boy in the bed beside him was shapelessly fat, wet his bed regularly, and cried in his sleep. When he had a chance, he made little balls of paper and ate them. He could rip them out of a forgotten magazine in the day room, from a sack that someone forgot on a table in the large dark hall. He scratched at the wallpaper down by the doorway until someone told him that you were not allowed to do that.

He used to feed the other boy paper occasionally himself. It was funny to see how quickly it disappeared.

You didn't get much pleasure from the boy in the bed on the other side. He was silent.

But the wallpaper, especially in the morning, with its faded blue and pink lines, the wallpaper was almost the only thing that comforted him. The lines crossed and went apart again, they formed images. You could make trees, large, complex trees with branches that forked off and then forked off again all the way up to the ceiling. You could let a tree represent another tree, so that there were two mirror trees opposite each other, each on its own wall, one in the shadow, the other in the sun.

He could lie for a long time and build trees, so that they thought he was sick in the morning.

He was just in the process of making a tree that represented itself inside itself when the aide came and got him to get up. She examined the sheet inquisitively.

He was among those who washed themselves. It was his custom to suck for a long time on the celluloid handle of the toothbrush.

The shoe knots were the worst. The knot was a little wicked animal that the lace ran through. Laces and knots were not the same thing, because you could make the same knot with many kinds of laces. His knots were always terribly complicated.

Spring came, and suddenly they were all sent home in a day. It was April of 1940, and the building was to be used for something else.

His mother came and praised him and said that he had grown.

Drank coffee with the aides, and it sounded like they were speaking with disguised voices.

At home the snow was melting, his brother and sister had grown much more than he had, and the old horse had died and lay buried near the pasture. He had never liked it. It had large, yellow, menacing teeth, it had a way of tossing its heavy head, in the half-light of the stall, which frightened him.

It was gone, and that was as it should be.

One week at home, he was on the verge of drowning in a brook when he went too far out on the loose edge of the ice, until he fell and got a good whipping.

It was his brother who pulled him up, one of his red boots remained in the slush; his brother poked around for a long time with a fence pole after the boot, while the boy stood beside him shivering. He cried, because he knew that the worst would be coming.

His nose was sore from the water; the water you take deep into your nose has a remarkable power to smart.

The first coltsfoot grew all the way up to his foot, which was heavy with mud. His nose was running, he was shaking from the cold. His thin overalls smelled damp, putrid from the brook's water; he stood completely still and freezing, and someone out there owed him endless love.

Not a trace of mushrooms in April.

In the spring of 1945, right near the end of the Second World War, he learned how to masturbate.

He thought he had made a fantastic discovery: he could surprise himself. He rubbed that very spongy thing, preferably toward the right side of the bed, and mused over his wallpaper tree, went at it all the more intensely, and had done it many times with ever increasing desire, an excitement, a feeling that the world became *closer* that way, when he discovered for the first time that it had an end. It frightened him the first time: his body knew something that he didn't know it knew. It was able to do something he had never thought it was able to.

How many secrets like that did it have? How many such new secret pockets could it open?

And was he unique in the world with regard to this? It was, in a way, the happiest spring of his life.

They made it clear to him that he was doing something forbidden, especially the older aides, who had a way of being disgusted with it. But they were not too strict. It belonged.

So he got himself a playmate, a mirror. He was no longer alone. He began to grow, got real tall. Mirror and mirror image grew together and could not be distinguished from one another. And yet they carried on their secret conversation. The trees in the wallpaper acquired depth.

During this period, approximately between 1945 and 1950, he was very close to something that could have been an awakening. He was moved to another room—without wallpaper—he stood in the door of the arts and crafts room and observed with interest those who were able to do woodwork.

A new teacher came, a lean, rather lanky young man with mild brown eyes, who in the beginning let him participate and straighten things up, sort out pieces of wood in the lumber supply room, who pretended he did not see the other pupils laughing at him.

He wasn't allowed to touch saws and chisels, but he was allowed to take part in the sandpapering, help hold when the glue clamps were to be put around the piece of work while the hot glue still bubbled in the pot.

The new teacher—he never learned his name—was almost as taciturn as he himself was. He moved with calm resolute steps between the tool cabinet and the benches, had the paint cans and lumber supply well organized. He always looked him in the eyes when he gave him a chore, a board to carry, a floor to sweep. He looked him in the eyes and showed that he was there. When he handed him a pail of shavings to be emptied it was a living sign, which told him that he existed.

The pupils in this workshop were of different sorts, also of different ages. A lot of things happened that scared him—as well as amused him. As clumsy as calves, older and younger boys moved around each other. There were jokes and taunting, glue pots in the hair and board ends that were nailed to the floor when you were supposed to pick them up. It bothered him and scared him when they were directed against him. The laughter was something they tried to force on him. The board on the floor was a trick they played on somebody whom they wanted him to be. But he wasn't there.

The new teacher knew how to subdue such things with a calm hand; without harsh words he separated those fighting when the boys were entangled and dragging each other around a bench with a firm grip in each other's hair.

Patiently he showed that you cannot plane a board in both directions without ripping up the fibers. He never allowed dirt to remain under his short-clipped, wide nails.

He was, in a way, the center of the world.

In a world that had no center he reigned like a quiet prince, oblivious to any threat to his own order, too rich to ask anything of the poor, an envoy in the midst of chaos for an order so noble that it could also accept the necessity of disorder.

There were those who urinated in the shaving pails when they weren't able to make it to the toilets inside the main entrance. They had to clean up themselves, but a harsh word was never spoken.

It was a little different with the female aides. They were so divided between disgust and motherliness, so pent up in a motherliness that was at the same time disgust, that they always caused anxiety. They smelled different. Their large white forearms, often fiery red, fascinated him, and he often tried to touch them, but was gently pushed away. He was "in the way," as it was called. He suspected great secrets in them, figured out that it was only a thin strip of their lives he saw, but was unable to formulate it. They changed, so often that there was no possibility to keep a face in the memory: as the years passed all of their faces merged into a single one, and it was mild and speechless.

He himself also glided away. The shop teacher moved after a couple of years; the workshop was discontinued, since those pupils who had worked there moved to another kind of institution. There were quite a few who disappeared, and only the hopeless remained.

The traffic along the road outside increased more and more with the years. In the spring of 1952 a big truck loaded with grain from the exchange got caught when it was trying to avoid a boy on a Husqvarna 125 cc; the trailer went down through the overly soft shoulder, and everything overturned in their hedge.

The driver climbed out, slightly injured, and saw two hydrocephalic boys wallow like small seals in the yellow grain that filled the entire ditch.

He thought he had landed in another world.

The salvage went quickly, but they scooped up wheat for weeks down by the ditch, played with it, filled their pockets. The aides found wheat under the beds, in the pillows, everywhere. It was a mysterious gift, and it came from the outside.

That was the last really big event for a long time. His senses slept: there was nothing that needed them enough. He lived for the meals and in his thirties became grotesquely fat. The blue carpenter's pants with their suspender clasps had to be let out.

The traffic along the road increased. He was always led across the road when he was going to help out in the apple orchard on the other side. He wasn't of much use. He walked around for the most part and raked, and not infrequently he raked under a single tree until the ground was all torn up and some laughing foreman came and moved him.

He had a deep fear of the motor-driven cultivator which came in 1956; one of the regular orchard workers had caught his foot in it that spring, and it looked dreadful, toes hanging loose, blood streaming out, but that wasn't what scared him, rather the helpless screams when everyone came running. After that he refused to remain in the orchard when the cultivator got moving and rushed back to the home, right across the road.

They let him go.

He didn't want to hear that scream again.

He had another peculiarity, too, that amused the men in the market garden: he was afraid of birds.

Not of birds that flew, not of flights of wild geese and cranes and common swifts that frolicked about high in the air on summer evenings. It was the birds that suddenly flew up from bushes which scared him; sparrows that fluttered up from a newly mowed field could make him absolutely beside himself with fear; even as a thirty-year-old he ran all the way into the kitchen in such situations, in spite of its being forbidden, and talked incomprehensibly.

Nice aides usually tried to comfort him with a piece of cake: he could sit for a long time, trembling and stiff, until the fear gradually left. He had no words for the world, and birds that suddenly flew up were one of the thousand ways in which the world could be *unreliable.*

The birds were not something that flapped through the world, the birds were a corner of the world's cover that had lost its hold and begun to flap.

Surely there was fear in that, but also liberation; that dream he dreamed would come to an end.

At the end of the '50s his parents died. No one tried to explain it to him, and he didn't know in which order they died, or when, but when he hadn't seen them in several years—his mother visited him regularly twice a year and always brought along candy and apples, many, many apples, as if a shortage of apples was his problem—he began to long for them, in an indefinite way, almost the way you can suddenly begin to long for mustard or honey or a certain kind of flour sauce with a faint aftertaste of burnt meat.

He remembered the buildings better than them; the horse, the woodshed; the only thing remaining of his parents was the sound of their closing the hall door and stamping the snow from their shoes in the winter. But this sound was an important sound. It meant that the lights were going to be lit, that the atmosphere in the room was going to change.

At the end of September every year the willow herbs and the rambler roses have no flowers left, but their seedcases ride on the wind, rise and fall rhythmically; they come into the farm at the slightest temperature change. And settle down finally in order, in small quick drifts, that the wind can easily take again.

And that's how September of 1977 was.

He was sitting in the day room in the new home, more than sixty miles from the old one, which had been torn down in 1963. He had his favorite spot by the window. And here there was an asphalt yard, without trees, without flowers, just a drooping flowerbed in the corner near the driveway and the three parking lots.

Here the seedcases of the willow herbs drifted in. It was one of those September days when the air *stands absolutely still and waits.* He was shapeless in the easy chair; he swelled out beyond its edges. For the past ten years or so he had been absolutely empty.

The drifting seedcases, unbelievably light, carried by breezes so slight that no one could discern them.

Slowly the shadow of the curtain shifts toward the waxed floor of the day room.

The hourglass-shaped belt of light moved over the planet's surface, the dawn line and the dusk line rushed forward like large wings over distant forests and mountains. Slowly or quickly, according to the measures you chose, the earth moved through its orbit and would never return to the same point where it once had been. Slowly or quickly, the solar system moved in its orbit, and with silent giddying speed like a discus of light the galaxy moved in its enigmatic self-rotation.

In their mothers' bodies yet unborn offspring grew, ingeniously membranes and tissues relaxed and crumpled around each other and explored without sorrow and without hesitation the topological possibilities of space.

He knew nothing about this: heavy and gigantic, like an erratic boulder in the forest, he sat in his chair and pushed it only with difficulty a few inches every hour, so that it remained in the sun streak the whole time. He was just as slow as the galaxy and just as enigmatic.

In the shadow of the foliage that moved more insistently toward the wall he saw the old mushrooms grow again, from the first soft batch that shoots through the moss to the last dark brown pyramids of formless, pungently smelling tissues in December.

For years he let them grow free when he sat here; he made them all the more visible, the more highly imaginative; each and every one of them the only one of its kind, saw them live and die and had known for a long time that all time, everything growing, was just as enigmatic and great as he himself.

NOTES ON CONTRIBUTORS

CAROL JANE BANGS lives with her husband and two children in Port Townsend, Washington, where she directs literature programs for the Centrum Foundation. New Directions published her first major collection, *The Bones of the Earth,* in 1983.

E. M. BEEKMAN is a professor of German and comparative literature at the University of Massachusetts, Amherst. His novels *Lame Duck* and *The Killing Jar* appeared in 1971 and 1976, respectively. He the general editor of *The Library of the Indies,* a twelve volume series of Dutch colonial literature in English translation, published by the University of Massachusetts Press. He published a translation of Paul van Ostaijen in *ND21* and two stories in *ND24* and *30*. A volume of his poetry was brought out this year by Pennyroyal Press.

Born in Rumania, ANDREI CODRESCU has for many years made his home in Baltimore. He is a columnist for the *Baltimore Sun,* an editor of the monthly *Exquisite Corpse,* and a commentator on National Public Radio's "All Things Considered." His autobiographical *The Life and Times of an Involuntary Genius* is available from George Braziller; a fiction, *In America's Shoes,* from City Lights; and *Selected Poems 1970–1980,* from Sun Books.

HUME CRONYN was born in London, Ontario, but has lived for the last ten years in London, England. His work has appeared in *Kayak, Ambit,* and elsewhere.

JOE FRANK's career in radio began in 1976, when he was the host for "In the Dark," an off-beat Saturday night comedy show on WBAI in New York. He soon moved on to become weekend anchor on National Public Radio's "All Things Considered," and since 1979, he has created radio dramas for NPR. These plays, which combine written and improvised material, have won two Armstrong Awards, a Broadcast Media Award, a Public Radio Program Award, and the Gold Award of the International Radio Festival of New York.

Poems by BARENT GJELSNESS have appeared in *Kayak, The Minnesota Review*, and *ND25*. He makes his home in Bisbee, Arizona.

Through his writings in mathematics, sociology, history, philosophy, and literature, LARS GUSTAFSSON's influence has been strong in all quarters of the European academic community. He has published in virtually every area of *belles lettres:* novels, stories, poetry, drama, literary criticism, and journalism. New Directions brought out his novels *The Death of a Beekeeper* (1981) *The Tennis Players* (1983), and forthcoming this winter is *Sigismund.* JOHN WEINSTOCK, translator of *Sigismund,* is associate dean of the College of Liberal Arts, the University of Texas at Austin, where Gustafsson has been a visiting professor for the last several years.

A professor at the University of Utah, ROBERT F. HELBLING is the author of *Heinrich von Kleist: The Major Works* (New Directions, 1975).

Nervous Songs, PAUL HOOVER's latest book of poems, is available from L'Epervier Press in Seattle. His earlier collections include *Somebody Talks a Lot* and *Letter to Einstein Begining Dear Albert,* both published by The Yellow Press, Chicago. He is co-director of The Poetry Center, a Chicago reading series, and edits *OINK!*, an annual literary magazine. A former NEA fellowship recipient, he has recently received an Artist's Grant in Poetry from the Illinois Arts Council.

DAVID HUERTA was born in Mexico City in 1949. Five collections of his verse have appeared in his native country, and he has been the recipient of a Guggenheim Fellowship. He is co-editor of *La Mesa*

Llena, a literary magazine, and works in Mexico City as an editor and translator. MAUREEN AHERN, a professor of Latin American literature at Arizona State University, was educated in Peru, where she was an editor of *Havarec*, a bilingual literary magazine. She is editor of the anthology *Peru: The New Poetry* (Red Dust, 1977), and her translation of Antonio Cisneros appeared in *ND43*.

Information about ROBERTO JUARROZ is found in the translator's introduction to his "Ten Poems." LOUIS BOURNE is an American living in Madrid, where his book of poems *Médula de la llama* won second prize in the Gules Competition. He has published translations of Vicente Aleixandre and others, many of which have appeared in these pages.

J. LAUGHLIN is president and publisher of New Directions. His *Stolen and Contaminated Poems* will be published this fall by Turkey Press (Santa Barbara) and another collection, *Nothing That's Lovely Can My Love Escape*, by City Lights in 1985.

RIKA LESSER's book of poems, *Etruscan Things*, was brought out by George Braziller in 1983. She has translated Hermann Hesse's *Hours in the Garden* (Farrar Straus & Giroux, 1979), and *Pictor's Metamorphoses & Other Fantasies* (Farrar, Straus & Giroux, 1979) from the German, and Gunnar Ekelöf's *Guide to the Underworld* (The University of Massachusetts Press, 1980) from the Swedish.

New Directions has published six books by MICHAEL MCCLURE, including his 1978 Obie Award-winning play *Josephine: The Mouse Singer* and, most recently, *Fragments of Perseus* (1983), a poetry collection. A book of essays, *Scratching the Beat Surface*, was brought out by North Point Press in 1982.

Born in Belgium in 1899, HENRI MICHAUX has lived for many years in Paris and the South of France. André Gide's essay "Découvrons Henri Michaux" helped to win a wide audience for his prose poems, sketches, free verse, and travelogs, many of which are included in *Selected Writings of Henri Michaux*, translated by Richard Ellmann (New Directions, 1968). This fall, New Directions will be bringing out Gustaf Sobin's translation of *Ideograms in China* as a signed, limited edition. GUSTAF SOBIN is an American poet living in Provençe who has published three collections: *Wind Chrysalid's Rattle* (Montemora, 1980), *Celebrations of the Sound Through* (Montemora, 1982), and *The Earth as Air* (New Directions, 1984).

ROBERT NICHOLS is the author of *Daily Lives in Nghsi-Altai*, a tetralogy brought out by New Directions between 1977 and 1979. His memoir in prose and poetry, "Clara Remembered," appeared in *ND46*.

JOYCE CAROL OATES is a renowned and prolific author of stories, poetry, nonfiction, and novels. Her latest collection of stories is *Last Days* (E. P. Dutton, 1984). She is an editor as well of The Ontario Review Press.

JOSÉ EMILIO PACHECO is one of Mexico's leading poets and fiction writers. Two of his books are available in the U.S.: *Don't Ask Me How the Time Goes By*, translated by Alastair Reid (Columbia University Press, 1978), and *Signals from the Flames*, translated by Thomas Hoeksema (Latin American Review Press, 1980). "The Amusement Park" is KATHERINE SILVER's first published translation.

Short fiction by CATHERINE PETROSKI has been collected in *Gravity and Other Stories*, and she holds an NEA Fiction Writing Fellowship for 1983–84. She is a professor at Duke University.

A collection of JOAN RETALLACK's poetry, *Circumstantial Evidence*, is being published this fall by S.O.S. Press. A recent essay in *Parnassus* won a Pushcart Prize, and she is currently at work on poetry, critical essays, and an extended fiction. Retallack is on the faculty of the Bard Institute for Writing and Thinking and teaches in the Honors Program at the University of Maryland.

BRIAN SWANN has published books of poetry, fiction, children's stories, and translations from the Italian, Greek, and Native American, as well as anthologies of Italian and Native American poetry. He is on the faculty of the Cooper Union in New York City.

In 1982–83, JULIA THACKER was a Bunting Fellow in Creative Writing at Radcliffe, and she was awarded an NEA grant for fiction in 1983. Her poetry and fiction have appeared in *Antaeus, Pushcart VI, Mademoiselle, Ms., The Massachusetts Review, Tendril, ND45,* and elsewhere.

JAMES WEILL is the publisher of the Elizabeth Press in New Rochelle, New York, which brings out new and classic fine editions.

Poems by DOUGLASS WENRICH have appeared in *Poetry Australia, The Bad Henry Review, Home Planet News, Other Stages, The Scranton Literary Review, The Pikestaff Forum,* and *Scanlan's Saloon Poetry Anthology*. His play, *Rags-Pape'-Rags,* was produced Off-Off-Broadway last December.